CALL THE WIND
MARIAH

A Story of Survival and Romance at Sea
in a Futuristic World Turned Upside Down

W.W. Hennemann

Call The Wind Mariah

Copyright © 2025 by W.W. Hennemann

Cover design by: 100Covers

Printed in the United States of America

Dystopian Future Press

Library of Congress Control Number: 2025922255

ISBN - 979-8-9930738-1-1 (ebook)
ISBN - 979-8-9930738-2-8 (paperback)

Contents

CHAPTER 1

November 2055,
Sea Isle City, NJ

G unfire again, time to retract the staircase and close the shutters, wait for the tide to come in. Corey Wells activated the switch and watched as the house became a fortress. He turned on the viewing screen and watched for the gradual approach of the sea. High tide was the safest time of day, a time when only those with access to a stilt house or a serviceable boat could survive in Sea Isle City.

Corey thought back to the good times, before the Tipping Point had been reached and the sea level rose. He and his family had loved their seaside home, living in harmony with nature and the vibrant Sea Isle community. Fishing, swimming, surfing, sailing—so many pleasures to enjoy and share. Little did he know that the lessons learned from his boyhood hobbies would become the key to his survival.

Corey knew that the situation in Sea Isle was no longer manageable. Sooner or later he would be surprised and/or overrun by a gang of mainlanders, and in the process lose his refuge, his food supply, and probably his life.

"I hate the thought of leaving Sea Isle City. I hate leaving the house that my parents built. It's the only home and community I have ever known," he said aloud in exasperation as if expecting the house to answer.

But there was no longer any reason to stay. Mom and Dad long passed. Sister hopefully still alive and safe in Bermuda.

"But I'd better get out now or join my parents in a watery grave," he said with resignation.

And the house did answer—with a groan, as the waves of the incoming tide began to swarm around the base of the house on stilts.

CHAPTER 2

Mariah

Corey lowered the dinghy from its davits and climbed on board. He activated the solar-powered aqua-jet motor and headed out to sea. His ticket out of the madness into which the United States had descended was anchored approximately one mile due east of his stilt house—the forty-five-foot sailing catamaran named *Mariah*.

Mariah, named for a century-old song that his father had loved to sing at the top of his lungs when sailing— "They call the Wind Mariah". The memory of his dad at the helm, his mom, sister and he tucked snuggly into the cockpit, skimming over the surface of the sea at speeds of ten to twelve knots, all singing the lyrics to this show tune from 1951 at the top of their lungs, made him smile. Life was wonderful before the Tipping Point had been reached. Now it was a struggle to survive.

Corey eased the dinghy up to *Mariah*'s port side and activated the security code, allowing him to board without being shocked back into the sea. He climbed aboard and cleated the painter of the dinghy to *Mariah*'s stern. Corey activated the solar-battery-powered winch hoisting the mainsail before deactivating the electromagnetic anchor. He gradually backed off the wind and eased *Mariah*'s bow toward shore, the computerized winches tugging on the sheets maintaining perfect trim to the sails.

It would be a short run to the house where Corey would tie *Mariah* off and load his provisions before the tide was able to recede. *Mariah*'s keels have sensors that would retract the keels and rudders and balance the weight throughout the boat, allowing for precise distribution of the ballast. This computerized AI-enabled system prevented the boat from capsizing even when the keels were retracted so that the boat could draw less than three feet in relatively calm seas. The water at the base of Corey's house was ten feet in depth at mean high tide, giving him plenty of clearance on a calm day like today to dock the boat for a few hours. This would be sufficient time to load the perishable provisions, the mobile garden that would provide vegetables and a source of vitamin C, and equipment too heavy to transport on the dinghy.

Fortunately, Amazon was still delivering to Sea Isle and the adjacent Ludlum Island community of Strathmere by drone. Corey had heard that this service would soon be limited to the large inland cities that had literally become islands of civilization in a sea of anarchy. The drones were frequently targets for bandits who would shoot them down and pilfer their contents. As such, it was becoming increasingly unprofitable to deliver food and essentials to remote locations such as Sea Isle. Corey took advantage of the service one final time to stock up for his trip into the unknown.

Once loaded, Corey would turn *Mariah* out to sea with the receding tide and begin his journey eastward, away from the United States and toward Bermuda.

CHAPTER 3

Setting Sail

Corey finished loading the last of the hydroponic tomatoes onto *Mariah*, turned and took one last look at his home. He was almost overwhelmed with sadness at the thought of leaving his beloved stilt home, probably never to return. However, the thought of reuniting with his baby sister Kelly and her new family in Bermuda was motivation enough to leave Sea Isle behind, as if the desire for self-preservation wasn't sufficient.

He closed *Mariah*'s hatches and prepared to shove off. The sun was just beginning to melt behind the mainland to the west. The moon had set hours before, so the night would be as black as jet.

November was not the ideal time for a crossing. Corey had wanted to wait until December when the threat of hurricanes had diminished and the winter storms that occasionally sweep down from the now frigid climes of New England

and Canada in January and February had yet to commence. But the violence of the mob was too close and too real to be ignored any more. It was time to go.

Corey would begin the journey under power from the solar-powered dual aqua-jet engine, without sail and without running lights. He did not want to venture more than a few miles offshore before darkness was in full effect.

Although the military had essentially conceded most of the country to the roving bands of thugs that had over-run it, they still maintained control of the seas within the twelve-nautical-mile territorial limit, meaning pirates and privateers were scarce until you were well at sea.

As Corey slowly left Ludlum Island, Sea Isle and Strathmere in his wake, he felt a sense of loss for the home and the lifestyle that had been so rich during his youth and early adulthood. His fear for the unknown dangers that lay ahead was tempered with excitement in anticipation of the new life that he planned to begin upon arrival in Bermuda with his baby sis and her family.

The seas began to increase, with ocean swells of three to five feet, still comfortable. The breeze began to freshen from the southwest as *Mariah* felt the effects of the Bermuda high that characteristically predominates the weather off the coast of New Jersey in November. It looked like a fairly smooth beam reach for the initial part of the voyage.

Corey raised the mainsail, turned off the aqua-jet and unfurled the jib; it was time to begin the journey in earnest.

Mariah's sails filled and the boat began to pitch rhythmically toward the edge of the blue water of the greatly diminished Gulf Stream.

Corey loved sailing at night in the open ocean—*Mariah*'s bow wave stimulating explosions of shimmering biolumines-cence from the ubiquitous zooplankton creating a mesmeriz-ing display of light, the occasional flying fish erupting from the ocean's surface and gliding away startled by the sudden appearance of a monstrous surface-skimming beast, the bril-liance of the sky illuminated by billions of stars, the occasion-al meteor shower, and the clearly visible cloud of light from Earth's home galaxy, the Milky Way. Yes, nighttime passages under calm seas were almost a religious experience.

Corey began to sing to himself. He enjoyed old folk songs and songs of the sea. The old songs were the best, espe-cially since the music industry had collapsed with the rest of society. The coastal cities that were vibrant hubs of the music and arts communities, including New York, Los Angeles, San Francisco, New Orleans and Miami, were inundated. Mass migrations and armed conflicts followed, culminating in the Sino-American war. Music was just another casualty of soci-ety's demise.

Yes, nighttime passages under calm seas were spiritu-ally uplifting with the majestic beauty of nature revealed in all its magnificence. Conversely, nighttime passages during a storm could be harrowing experiences—huge waves bat-tering the boat, violently tossing the vessel and its crew, rain pouring down so heavily that visibility is reduced to zero, lightning crashing and peals of thunder rattling the boat and the nerves. Any soul unlucky enough to be caught in such a tempest must either retreat into the cabin below decks or tether him/herself to the boat so as to not be washed overboard or cast into the sea. Such storms are to be avoided if at all possible, but without any reliable weather forecasts since the dismantling of NOAA and the National Weather Service, sailors are forced to rely on their own instincts and seamanship when taking long voyages at sea, and ideally to avoid sailing during hurricane season. Marine radar mounted on *Mariah*'s mast can detect storms at a range of approximately twenty miles, which is a valuable tool in avoiding and potentially outrunning squalls. However, mast-mounted radar is of little use in avoiding a massive storm like a hurricane.

Hurricane season extends from May through early December due to the warmer seas and the diminished flow of the once mighty Gulf Stream. Winter storms are common in late January through April. The ideal timing for extended Atlantic Ocean voyages is limited to December, early January and late April. Even during these relatively quiet periods, a monstrous storm could appear seemingly out of nowhere.

Unfortunately, the deteriorating situation at home, with rampant lawlessness and the occasional drone strike targeted at the gangs but sometimes resulting in collateral damage to innocent citizens and their homes, made it more dangerous to remain in Sea Isle than to chance a crossing during hurricane season.

CHAPTER 4

Navigating the Bermuda Triangle

There are approximately 600 nautical miles separating Sea Isle and Bermuda. Catamarans like *Mariah* can average anywhere between eight to fifteen knots depending on the conditions. Whereas in earlier years the Gulf Stream flowed from southeast to northwest across the Atlantic with a surface current velocity of up to six knots, the modern Gulf Stream in November 2055 averages one knot across its breadth.

Satellite navigation is spotty as most of the satellites were destroyed in the Sino-American war. As such, Corey must rely on his skill in navigating using dead reckoning. Corey plotted a course using a well-worn nautical chart. He estimated the impact of the Gulf Stream current, the speed of the boat, and the potential impact of the prevailing southwesterly winds to draw a rhumb line on the chart. He would sail a course heading of 115° for approximately seventy hours to reach Bermuda, assuming no untoward weather events along the way. Corey set the autopilot and headed to his berth below decks as the boat skipped along toward the southeast at a brisk ten knots.

Mariah was fitted with the latest in technology, including forward-looking sonar connected to the robotic autopilot enabled with artificial intelligence. The autopilot can detect changes to the wind and adjust the trim of the sails to optimize performance and/or maintain a desired cruising speed. The forward-looking sonar is able to detect debris in the water—flotsam and jetsam—and change course to avoid them. Floating debris had always been a potential hazard to navigation, especially at night. The problem was magnified several-fold by the massive fields of debris created as entire cities were submerged under the ever-rising tides. The AI-enabled autopilot and forward-looking sonar gave Corey peace of mind as he drifted off to sleep.

Corey's respite was short-lived. He awoke with a start to the sound of an engine approaching from the south. The sun was just beginning its climb above the horizon to the southeast. The sky was a shimmering virtually cloudless blue, perfect weather for day one of his adventure at sea.

The approaching boat was definitely cause for alarm however. Encounters with pirates were not uncommon in the area known as the Bermuda Triangle. Powerboats could match or exceed *Mariah*'s speed, and would be able to over-take and out maneuver a boat under sail.

Damn, could be pirates. Time to become a speedboat. Corey activated *Mariah*'s auxiliary hydrogen fuel cell bat-tery-powered dual jet engine and steered *Mariah* into the wind. He quickly lowered and furled the sails, retracting them automatically into the mast. *Mariah*'s hydrogen fuel cell battery was able to sustain only relatively short runs, but under power the catamaran can do a top speed of thirty knots. The approaching boat was a monohull design and unlikely to keep pace with a speeding cat. Although it's possible that the approaching boat was not a threat, Corey didn't want to risk it. He thought he could outrace the monohull before the battery ran out of power and he had to convert back to sail.

Corey knew that he would have to change course to put distance between *Mariah* and the monohull. Even if he escaped the apparent danger, he would have to estimate his location and recalculate his course to compensate for the deviation. He could potentially be lost at sea. That concern paled in comparison to the more immediate threat now bear-ing down on him.

Corey called out "Come on baby, let's run" as he steered *Mariah* northward, away from the oncoming boat. The sounds of distant gunfire erupted as *Mariah* kicked into power mode and began to pull away from the powerboat. Splashes erupted in the sea around *Mariah* as bullets fired from the pirate boat missed their mark. Corey accelerated to thirty-five knots, stressing the limits of *Mariah*'s auxiliary engine. He could see the pirate boat fading into the distance behind him and knew that he had made the right decision to flee. "Man, that was close," Corey exclaimed.

It appears that storms and inclement weather were not the only perils that he would have to contend with on his journey toward a new and hopefully better life in Bermuda.

CHAPTER 5

Off Course

Corey ran due north for an hour until his fuel cell battery was almost ninety percent depleted. By then the pirate boat was no longer visible on the horizon. He turned the engine to idle and bobbed in the water as he tried to estimate his location and re-plot a course to Bermuda.

Corey did not own or know how to use a sextant. He would have to rely again on dead reckoning to estimate his location and his course. He assumed that his run took him thirty-six nautical miles north of his previous rhumb line. Corey estimated the location where he began his northward run and his new location on the chart using his drafting compass. He estimated the distance to Bermuda, the potential impact of wind and current, and drew a new rhumb line to Bermuda. The escape from the pirates had set him well off course. The prevailing winds were now less in his favor and he would have to hold a course closer to the wind. He was still an estimated sixty-five hours from his destination.

Corey once again steered *Mariah* into the wind, re-deployed the sails and renewed his journey. Hopefully he would not encounter any more pirates, as his hydrogen-powered battery was nearly depleted and his solar battery-powered aqua-jet could only sustain a maximum speed of fifteen knots. The wind however was brisk and the speedy cat was once again on course and making good time.

CHAPTER 6

Sailing Solo

Corey awoke to another dazzling sunrise. The eastern sky was ablaze with brilliant hues of red and orange as the sun began its ascent into the powder blue sky. "Another beautiful day, hopefully my luck will hold," Corey muttered to himself. Sailors have always been a superstitious lot, and Corey was no exception. He wondered if he hadn't just jinxed himself. "Time for a caffeine fix," as he opened another can of synthetic vanilla latte.

Actual coffee had become an actual luxury. Plants of the genus coffea, whose berries produce the seeds that are roasted and ground to make the aromatic and stimulating beverage known as coffee, require specific conditions including warm temperatures, high humidity and indirect sunlight to thrive. These conditions historically were found only in tropical and subtropical climates, often at elevation. Optimal conditions for the cultivation of coffee became harder and harder to meet as climate change accelerated toward the Tipping Point, and coffee growing became increasingly difficult and unprofitable. When the price of coffee became out of reach for most, a synthetic beverage of similar taste and quality was developed to meet the demand. It had been years since Corey had tasted actual coffee, which he greatly preferred over this synthetic swill. Even when available, it can be difficult to brew coffee in a pitching sailboat, so the canned synthetic beverage would have to do. Corey never started the day without at least one canned synthetic coffee beverage, followed by a trip to the head for a morning constitutional.

An extra dose of caffeinated beverage was definitely required after approximately five hours of restless sleep. Sleeping at sea was always challenging, with frequent fits of wakefulness due to anxiety or when the motion of the boat shifted due to an occasional larger than average wave. This challenge was exacerbated when you are the only crew member and there is no one to relieve you to take the midnight watch.

Rogue waves are not uncommon in the modern ocean, even during relatively calm three to five-foot seas. Corey recalled a sailing trip in a monohull sloop crossing the Florida Straits from Ft. Lauderdale to the Bahamas with his family when he was twelve years old, before the Tipping Point had been reached and the Gulf Stream had slowed to a relative trickle. The Wells family was sailing with two other families for a week-long excursion to Bimini and the Berry Islands, situated on the edge of the Great Bahama Bank—a massive shallow sea surrounded by much deeper waters including the abyss known as the Tongue of the Ocean.

Crossing the Gulf Stream in a sailing vessel was typically done at night, so as to make landfall in the morning after a ten-hour sail in favorable winds. The winds on this passage however shifted to the southeast in the middle of the night, and all three vessels lowered sail and engaged their diesel engines in an attempt to make progress in the face of a freshening headwind. After hours making little headway beating into an increasingly angry sea, two of the boats decided to sail eastward toward the Bahama Bank and then tack south to reach safe harbor. The skipper of the third boat elected to continue beating into the wind and waves under power.

Sailing eastward not only allowed the sloops to make better time, approaching seven knots, but also took the boats out of the axis of the Gulf Stream where the current could be almost four knots. Both boats reached safe harbor in the lee of an uninhabited Bahamian island by the middle of the next day. By that time the winds were gale force and the seas at least eight to ten feet.

The sailboat that had elected to motor on without changing course lost power due to a vapor lock in the engine. They raised sail and attempted to sail to safety in the face of dramatically worsening conditions. As night fell they had yet to reach land, seasick and weakened due to the extended voyage in unexpectedly horrible conditions. A rogue wave took out the mainsail and knocked the boat down, washing a family member overboard. Although the boat eventually made it to safety with help of a Coast Guard vessel, the body of the seasick woman washed into the sea was never recovered. That experience left a lasting impression on Corey, and he consequently always tethers himself to the boat in all but the calmest seas, especially when sailing alone. Corey would not have a restful night's sleep until he was safely at anchor in a protected harbor.

CHAPTER 7
Catch of the Day

As the November sun climbed higher into the sky, Corey began to feel pangs of hunger. Tired of munching on prepackaged rations, he decided to try his luck at catching fresh fish for lunch. Corey grew up fishing and crabbing in the local waters around Sea Isle. His dad, sister and he caught fresh sea bass, flounder and blue crab on a regular basis during his youth, and his mom was an expert at preparing savory seafood dishes including blackened fish, fish meuniere, crab cakes and paella. Although Corey knew how to fillet and prepare fish for dinner, he could never match or even approach his mother's culinary magic.

"Man, what I wouldn't give for Mom's blackened mahi right now," Corey said as he rummaged in the locker for his fishing gear. His beloved parents had long since passed, killed by an errant strike from an AI-enabled autonomous drone while traveling inland by car to purchase provisions. Corey never fully recovered from losing them, and their memory brought a tear to his eye.

Although the stocks of pelagic fish had been sorely depleted due to overfishing and ever-warming waters, schools of mahi mahi, also known as dorado or dolphin fish, could still be found in the open ocean. In fact, stocks of certain pelagic fish species, such as mahi, had somewhat recovered as the human population was in decline and commercial fishing in many areas was too dangerous due to the increasingly violent and unpredictable storms and the risk of piracy. The flooding of the cities had released many toxins into the water. Shellfish and many fish species, especially bottom-feeding fish, were unsafe to consume. Pelagic fish, such as the mahi mahi, were still safe to eat in small quantities, assuming you could find them.

Corey choked back the wave of grief over his lost parents and rigged two lines with fishing lures. He shortened sail to reduce speed to seven knots, a reasonable trolling speed without sacrificing too much headway toward Bermuda. He knew that he would need to adjust course as a result, but the lure of a fresh fish dinner was too appealing to pass up.

After an hour of trolling, Corey noticed a sizable patch of sargassum floating ahead and slightly to port. Sargassum rafts are an ecosystem unto themselves, providing shelter for smaller fish, crabs, squid and other marine species that are prey to mahi mahi. Experienced fishermen take advantage of this knowledge, cruising the margins of sargassum rafts in hopes of encountering a school of mahi. Corey steered *Mariah* slightly to port so that the fishing lines trailing behind the boat would pass adjacent the floating weed. "There are mahi here" Corey exclaimed as he observed fish leaping out of the water excitedly as they pursued the bait.

Corey's family always loved fishing for mahi mahi. Besides being delicious to eat, they were among the most exciting fish to catch. Dolphin fish are fast, aggressive and acrobatic. They will vigorously leap from the water and large ones will run at high speed away from the boat after taking the bait. Corey and his dad once encountered a large school of dolphin feeding on sardines in open water. The fish were in an excited frenzy and would hit anything shiny, even an unbaited hook dragged or reeled through the water. They each caught their limit of ten fish in approximately ten minutes before heading home for a delicious feast of fresh mahi.

"Fish on," Corey yelled as a large fish leaped aggressively from the surface, flashing shades of green, blue, silver and yellow. The powerful bull mahi began his run away from the boat, rapidly taking line from the now screaming reel. Corey steered *Mariah* into the wind and reduced sail. He grabbed the rod out of the rod holder and began reeling in his catch, taking care not to exert too much force so as to potentially lose his prize in the process. Eventually the large male dorado weakened from the fight, was reeled to *Mariah*'s transom and brought aboard with the aid of a large landing net. It would be fresh fish for dinner today after all. In fact, the big bull would provide meat for several days.

After landing his catch, Corey reeled in the other line and stowed the fishing gear into the storage locker. *Well that was a worthwhile and pleasant distraction. Maybe I'll wait until after dinner to resume full sail,* Corey thought. The seas were relatively calm, two to four feet at present, and the catamaran's dual hull design provided more stability than a monohull would in such waters. He decided to prepare dinner without raising sail.

Mariah's galley was functional, but not elaborate. Corey filleted the mahi, carved out a nice portion for dinner, and placed the remaining several pounds of meat into a sealed container and into the small onboard refrigerator. He pan-fried the fish, plated it and left the cabin for the cockpit where he hungrily devoured the delicious meal. It was by far the best meal he had had in weeks.

After dinner it was time to wash the dishes and clean up the galley. Corey placed the frying pan, plate, filleting knife, and utensils into a mesh bag and heaved it over the transom. Fresh water was in limited supply on board, and cleaning and bathing had to be performed with salt water. In a cabinet in the galley Corey found an old half bottle of Joy detergent. Joy was the sailor's choice for such chores since it actually suds in salt water as well as fresh. Corey hauled the mesh bag back onto the boat, cleaned the contents in the galley's sink, and tossed them back overboard to rinse. As it had been a few days since he himself had bathed, Corey stripped off his clothes, tossed and secured a life preserver tethered by a six-meter rope line to a cleat on the stern, grabbed the bottle of Joy and dove off of the transom.

Offshore water is the deepest blue anyone can imagine. There is almost nothing more beautiful than the cobalt blue color of the deep ocean contrasted with the white of ocean foam as the waves lap against the side of the boat. That being said, it is always unnerving to plunge into these waters. Although the chances of encountering a pelagic shark was exceedingly unlikely, the subconscious mind cannot fully suppress the thought that a giant mako or great white shark would rise from the depths and strike a human as they would a seal or dolphin. Corey quickly lathered, rinsed and scrambled up the ladder back onto the boat, all the while glancing behind him to make sure that no giant predator was closing in on him. He knew that the fear was irrational, but there is something primal about it, and Corey was never able to fully shake it. He pulled the mesh bag onto the deck, quickly rinsed off its contents with a small amount of fresh water, and returned to the cockpit.

The sun was just beginning its descent toward the horizon in the west, filling the sky with beautiful streaks of color. "Time for another guestimate and course correction" Corey said out loud. After reviewing the chart and estimating his location, he modified his course and once again set sail toward Bermuda. Corey looked closely to the west as the sun dipped below the horizon, hoping to see the green flash.

CHAPTER 8

Red Sky in the Morning

Another restless night, another peaceful dawn. Corey looked to the east as the sun began to peak above the horizon. The early morning sunrise illuminated the cirrus clouds now appearing in the eastern sky, creating a dazzling display of reds and oranges.

"Uh oh," Corey muttered aloud. "Could be my luck with the weather has run out." The ancient biblical adage, "red sky at night sailors delight, red sky in morning sailors take warning," although not always accurate, has a scientific basis. Weather patterns in the middle latitudes, north of the Tropic of Cancer and south of the Arctic Circle wherein both New Jersey and Bermuda are located, tend to move west to east due to the prevailing westerly winds.

The climate has been dramatically altered by the precipitous melting of the glaciers, the Greenland ice sheet, and both the Arctic and Antarctic ice caps, with a consequent dramatic weakening of the once mighty Gulf Stream. The direction of the prevailing winds however, although certainly more variable and less predictable, remain fundamentally un-altered. The prevailing westerlies are the result of the Coriolis effect from the Earth's rotation combined with the rising and sinking of air masses from the uneven heating of the Earth as the direct rays of the sun continue their timeless migration from the Tropic of Cancer to the Tropic of Capricorn and back again in the course of Earth's journey around the sun. A red sky at night indicates that the oblique rays of the set-ting sun are being scattered by light clouds of dust particles and crystals of ice unobstructed by opaque heavy clouds ap-proaching from the west. As such, there is a high probability of fair weather ahead. Alternatively, the dawn's first rays may cast a reddish hue as they illuminate clouds heavily laden with moisture and high-level cirrus clouds that may be a har-binger of a weather front and foul weather approaching.

Corey anxiously checked the masthead radar for signs of an approaching storm. Sure enough, an unmistakable image appeared on the screen with large patterns of yellow and red indicating areas of moderate and heavy precipitation. This was no summer squall as he had experienced frequently while sailing as a kid. This was a massive storm that would sorely test Corey's seamanship and *Mariah*'s seaworthiness.

The leading edge of the storm was approximately nine-teen miles due northwest of Corey's position. The wind was already beginning to freshen out of the west. Although

Corey's course was southeasterly, away from the storm, Corey doubted that he could outrun the approaching storm and began to prepare for rough weather ahead.

Corey went below and stowed any loose gear or equipment. He retracted and secured the Bimini top that provided cover from the scorching rays of the sun and periods of rain while in the cockpit. While the Bimini top would provide some shelter from the rain, it is susceptible to damage in high winds, and can act like a sail in heavy weather making the boat less stable. He checked and secured the hatches and donned his foul weather gear and inflatable life jacket/personal flotation device. Finally, he prepared a tether to attach himself to *Mariah* during the impending tempest.

Soon it was not necessary to use radar to see the approaching storm. Dark, cumulonimbus clouds were rapidly overtaking the fleeing catamaran and whitecaps dotted the once tranquil surface of the sea. Faint flashes of lightning followed by rumbles of distant thunder were now apparent. "This is not going to be fun," Corey muttered shaking his head.

Although Corey long ago lost his faith in organized religion, he felt a connection to the natural world, and a hope, if not belief, that there was a spiritual force or a higher power connecting the living with the dead and the universe as a whole. Although the concept of a personal God having a plan for each and every soul on Earth seemed illogical and without evidence, especially given the misery that was apparent in so much of man's world, Corey wanted to believe in something more, and prayed daily as a result. Today would be no exception. Corey prayed to this spiritual force to help him survive the test that he was soon to face.

Corey did not trust the autopilot to handle *Mariah* in the storm. He disengaged the robot and took control of the helm. Before the storm was fully upon him, Corey activated the aqua-jet engine and steered *Mariah* into the wind so as to furl the sails and retract them once more into the mast. A small area of the mainsail remained unfurled. This would act as a trysail to add stability while relying on the engine to provide forward motion and mobility. The solar battery-powered engine has no carburetor or fuel line, so there would be no risk of vapor lock or similar mechanical failure as Corey's sailing companions had experienced during the ill-fated trip to the Bahamas during Corey's youth. *Mariah's* engine would not fail as long as the battery had power.

The waves were dramatically increasing in height, approaching eight to ten feet as the storm descended on *Mariah*. Rain lashed the deck as the winds approached gale force. The once beautiful deep blue sea and powder blue skies had been replaced by shades of angry grey. Visibility was near zero, and Corey was glad that he was outside of any traditional shipping lanes, as there would be no way to avoid collision with another boat in this maelstrom.

Corey steered the sturdy catamaran at an approximately forty-five-degree angle to the waves to minimize their impact and maximize his ability to control the helm. The storm had produced confused seas in which not all waves were traveling in the same direction, spawning a chaotic maelstrom that was difficult and exhausting to navigate. Corey struggled with the helm as *Mariah* took blow after blow from the massive waves that continually washed over her.

Mariah's single helm is raised-mounted in the cockpit, offset slightly to starboard. Although offering excellent visibility to all four corners of the boat and excellent for fair weather sailing, the cockpit location exposes the helmsman to the elements in heavy weather. Grey water and white foam filled and then drained from the cockpit after each collision with an ocean swell. The deck was awash with seawater, sometimes arriving with such power as to knock Corey off of his feet and (if not for his tether) wash him overboard. Spray and driving rain filled the air. Lightning flashed overhead while thunder shook the small vessel and her one-man crew. The hum from *Mariah*'s powerful bilge pumps, capable of pumping 4,000 gallons per hour from her bilge, could be heard even above the din of the storm as they worked continuously to keep her from being swamped with seawater.

Although catamarans are more stable in general, they have one huge disadvantage over a monohull in rough seas. In the event of a knockdown from a large or rogue wave, the monohull will right itself, whereas the cat will not. Successfully navigating this storm was a matter of life and death. If *Mariah* were to capsize there would be no Coast

Guard rescue. Even if he could reach the United States Coast Guard on the marine radio, their forces were spread very thin and he was well outside of the twelve-mile territorial limit patrolled by these brave lifesaving men and women. He was too far from Bermuda for any help from their navy. Corey had to overcome this trial by water without assistance, or be doomed to drift at sea until he ultimately succumbed to starvation, dehydration or drowning from the truly unsurvivable weather that would eventually follow with the onset of the winter storm season.

As the storm peaked in intensity, *Mariah* was battered by ten to twelve-foot waves and winds gusting in excess of fifty knots. *Mariah*'s lightning protection system, including a marine surge protector to shield her electronics, was tested under extreme field conditions as the boat was struck not once, but twice by lightning.

Corey stood at the helm, battling the angry sea and howling winds for over two hours until gradually, thankfully, he had maneuvered *Mariah* through the worst of the storm. The waves and wind began to subside in fury and intensity. Corey felt the flood of adrenaline that had carried him through the crisis begin to subside. He thanked his guardian angel or whatever force had guided him through the tempest—whether supernatural, pure luck, or the force of one man's courage and will. His seamanship and *Mariah*'s sturdy design had ultimately proved up to the task. He had survived trial by water and was grateful to be alive.

As the wind and waves diminished, Corey once again pointed *Mariah* into the wind to unfurl the mainsail. *Mariah*'s mainsail caught the wind and began to fall off. Corey unfurled the jib and once again set course toward Bermuda. *Mariah* proceeded in a southeasterly course under shortened sail as the winds were still gusting in excess of twenty knots with four to six-foot seas. *Mariah* was now however sailing downwind with following seas, a much more comfortable tack. The wind and seas continued to calm with the passing of the storm and Corey once again breathed a sigh of relief. Exhausted by the ordeal, he stripped off his foul weather gear, hungrily gobbled down two protein bars, drank a bottle of flavored electrolyte solution and retired to the aft starboard cabin for a well-earned nap. *Mariah* would be steered by robot until Corey was able to return to the watch.

CHAPTER 9

Reflection

Corey awoke with a start. He groggily rolled out of the bunk, staggered through the cabin, and climbed into the cockpit. Night had fallen, the skies had cleared and a crescent moon was rising in the east. Although the winds had diminished, they were still moderate to fresh. *Mariah* was maintaining excellent headway, with a cruising speed of almost fifteen knots toward the southeast. The boat swayed gently back and forth as the ocean swells now rocked *Mariah* from her stern and port quarters.

The beauty of the night, with only *Mariah*'s masthead and running lights to distract from the moon and the billions of pin-points of starlight that fill the night sky, was in stark contrast to the storm that had passed—a storm that had thankfully spared *Mariah* and its one-man crew.

Corey relaxed in the cockpit and treated himself to one of the few beers that he had been able to procure before his departure. He preferred strong beers, ales and porters, as opposed to the light beers and even stronger IPAs that were in vogue. Even as society itself was largely in disarray, there were still pockets of civilization where beer was brewed, food was raised, and people lived in relative safety. While sipping his cold beer and enjoying the peaceful downwind sail, Corey reflected on the unprecedented circumstances that led him to be alone on a sailboat in the middle of the Gulf Stream on a journey into the unknown.

As the glaciers, ice sheets and ice caps melted, including the Thwaites (or "Doomsday") Glacier and the West Antarctic Ice Sheet, coastlines began to move miles inland. The melting of the freshwater Greenland Ice Sheet and Arctic ice pack significantly impacted the salinity of the North Atlantic. Fresh water is less dense than sea water and will, therefore, be less likely to sink. It is the mass sinking of cold seawater and its replacement by warm water flowing from the south that is the engine for the Gulf Stream's circulation. As this engine was disrupted by the reduced salinity, the Gulf Stream abruptly weakened with catastrophic effects to the climate. The intensity of storms increased. England, Ireland, central and especially northern Europe cooled. Rainfall patterns were disrupted globally, including the monsoons that are critical for agriculture in heavily populated South Asia. Sea levels, especially along the east coast of North America, rose dramatically. Salt water infiltrated coastal aquifers contaminating drinking water and water used for irrigation. The

Tipping Point for global climate catastrophe was reached as the ocean conveyer belt slowed to a relative trickle.

Major coastal cities were inundated by the ten-foot rise in sea level, far greater and far sooner than the climate models had anticipated. The models had underestimated the effect of the many positive feedback loops affecting the climate, leading to runaway global warming once the Tipping Point had been reached. Melting of the permafrost near the poles released methane, a more powerful greenhouse gas than carbon dioxide. The more methane was released, the higher the temperatures, the faster the permafrost melted—a positive feedback loop. As the polar ice caps melted, less sunlight was reflected and more was absorbed by the oceans causing the oceans to warm further. The faster the oceans warmed the more ice melted, the less sunlight was reflected—a positive feedback loop. Forest fires raged throughout much of the temperate zones across the globe releasing huge amounts of carbon dioxide into the atmosphere. Higher temperatures increased the number and intensity of fires, which released more carbon dioxide, which led to increased temperatures, which in turn increased the risk of more fires—another positive feedback loop.

The final contributing factor was a lack of appreciation as to how critical the ocean was to mitigating the impact of greenhouse gas emissions on the terrestrial climate. From the onset of the industrial age to modern times the ocean has served as a buffer against global warming, absorbing much of the heat and carbon dioxide generated by human activity. However, there is a limit to the ocean's ability to absorb heat and CO_2. Global warming and climate change accelerated as the ocean's limits to absorb heat and carbon dioxide were approached.

Large areas of the world, including the southern and southwestern United States— most of Texas, New Mexico, Arizona, Nevada and Southern California—were essentially uninhabitable due to the intense summer heat and sporadic torrential rains leading to flash floods and mudslides. Heat waves where the temperatures never drop below a wet bulb temperature of 35° C (95° F) lasting weeks at a time were common. As the human body cannot cool itself under these conditions, the only way to survive is to remain indoors under air conditioning and to pray that there is no power outage. This, coupled with the lack of accessible potable water, made life in what was now an expansive desert extremely difficult or virtually impossible.

The frequent periods of torrential rains were often interspersed with extended periods of extreme drought. Crops in many formerly fertile regions of the world, including the American Midwest, began to fail. Crops failed not only because of the drought, but because excessive heat inhibits photosynthesis. The enzymes that play a critical role as catalysts in the chemical reactions of photosynthesis, the process through which plants convert the energy from sunlight into chemical energy consuming carbon dioxide and releasing oxygen, are at first inhibited and ultimately completely in-activated/denatured as temperatures climb above 35°C. The threat and ultimately the realization of famine lead to wide-spread panic and chaos.

Although many died, many more migrated to the north and inland leading to the displacement of many of the pre-vious residents, frequently at the point of a gun. City-states formed with well-armed police and military to protect the citizens of these newly incorporated municipalities from the lawlessness that ruled outside of the city-state proper. Small groups of coastal residents like Corey, who had the means and the wherewithal, were able to hang on by creating their own island of homes—elevated fortresses that stood tall above the rising sea and protected from the lawlessness by this fact alone. The sea provided protein in the form of fish, crabs and other shellfish. Some produce, including tomatoes, peppers, strawberries and beans, could be grown in small rooftop gar-dens or hydroponically. Seaweeds could be dried and eaten to augment the diet. Other provisions, including beer, could be ordered remotely and delivered by drone. Wifi had all but ceased to exist once the satellites went down, so landlines had been resurrected. People adapted to survive.

It was a lonely existence however, and Corey was tired of being alone. He was willing to risk it all to find a new life in the island nation of Bermuda. Many island nations across the globe were completely inundated making them virtually uninhabitable. In many cases their populations were relocated, often to other areas of the world that quickly became equally uninhabitable. Bermuda however had anticipated the global catastrophe to come, and had made the preparations necessary to survive it.

Bermuda was an archipelago of over 180 islands. Although many of the smaller islands and islets had been inundated, Bermuda was largely buffered from the worst effects of climate change. The climate was mild, and the frequent rains provided a ready source of fresh water. The six larger islands were now home to many who had had the foresight and sufficient wealth to flee there. It had become increasingly apparent to the educated and to those who refused to deny reality despite the ignorance and denial of their governments and the media that they largely controlled, that the Tipping Point would be reached and that the "new normal" would be catastrophe. The government of Bermuda not only took advantage of the influx of scientists, engineers, and people of means, they actively recruited them.

The islands are naturally protected from strong storms by the extensive reefs that surround them and by the fact that the most powerful hurricanes tend to weaken before they reach Bermuda due to wind shear from the jet stream, which now dips further south in both summer and winter. They strengthened their defenses against the rising seas, building a series of large dikes, sea walls and storm surge barriers. They built up their police and military and began restricting immigration in preparation for the likely crush of people who wanted to flee to a protected island refuge as chaos and violence descended and civilization retreated in many parts of the world.

Corey's sister Kelly and her husband, both medical professionals, had been among the first to emigrate. As longtime residents of Sea Isle, they saw the effects of climate change almost daily as the beach eroded and the tides penetrated further and further inland with each passing year, even before the Tipping Point. They read the writing on the wall, and, as relatively wealthy people with highly desirable skills, they were welcomed.

Corey, however, had a steady girlfriend in Sea Isle. In better times they would have been engaged or married. Corey loved her and had even bought wedding rings in anticipation. But modern times were not conducive to starting families. Corey also loved the house that his parents had constructed and designed to protect the family from the increasingly hostile elements as the sea rose higher and higher and the storms became stronger and more frequent.

Life on Sea Isle, however, ultimately became too difficult and too dangerous for his girlfriend and her family. They decided to escape by sailing south to the remnants of the federal district and surrounding Maryland and Virginia suburbs, a city-state that was well armed and well protected. Corey decided not to join them. Mistakes made in Washington had contributed greatly to the demise of the country that he once loved, and frankly to the world that he still loved. The former leaders of the country had ignored the threat of climate change, in fact actively denied it out of ignorance or for profit. They controlled the media and the narrative, did nothing to mitigate the risks, and ultimately lead the country into the Sino-American war over access to the Arctic and its mineral resources. Most of those responsible had either perished or fled, however Corey was not one to forgive and forget. Although neither side in the war had the sense to recognize climate change as the real and common enemy, at least both sides had the sense not to deploy nuclear weapons. The world had changed dramatically for the worse, but at least there was still a remnant of a world to inhabit for those fortunate enough to survive and with the fortitude to carry on.

CHAPTER 10

Mayday

Corey's reverie was interrupted shortly after midnight by a light flashing in the distance off *Mariah*'s port bow. According to his chart and his dead reckoning he was still approximately 250 nautical miles from the closest land, Bermuda. It could be a vessel, although no running lights were visible. Corey took out his binoculars and peered at the light. He could now detect a repeating pattern—three short flashes, followed by three longer flashes, followed once again by three short flashes. Corey was trained as a first responder and understood well that this signal meant "SOS", the now archaic Morse code precursor to the universal distress call "Mayday".

The term "Mayday" is derived from the French *m'aider*, loosely translated as "help me." Whatever its derivation, any sailor knows that the international law of the sea and an inviolable maritime custom is to respond to a Mayday and to aid any vessel in distress. Corey shortened sail, altered course, and began his approach toward the flashing light.

As *Mariah* drew closer to the still flashing beacon, Corey turned off his running lights and the masthead light. He fully furled the sails and activated the aqua-jet. As a solar-powered battery-driven EV engine, any sound that the aqua-jet made would be easily concealed by the ambient noise of wind and wave. Corey was wary of pirates and concerned that this could be a trap. As such, he wanted to make his approach as stealthy as possible.

The crescent moon provided little illumination, so Corey had to motor to within approximately 100 meters before he could identify the source of the distress signal. There dead in the water ahead was what appeared to be a catamaran that had capsized and turned turtle, floating upside down in the water. Corey could barely make out the form of what appeared to be a woman standing upon the turtled hull. Another form, that of a man, was prostrate beside her. The Mayday signal was not a decoy. This was not a pirate ambush, but was an actual vessel in distress. Although Corey was not sure he had sufficient provisions on board for three, he had no choice but to rescue the crew of the disabled and capsized boat. To do otherwise would condemn them, as the chances of encountering another vessel before they succumbed to dehydration or drowning in another storm was slim.

Corey carefully maneuvered *Mariah* alongside the capsized catamaran. He turned his deck lights on to provide some illumination for the task at hand. It would be difficult to raft up with a capsized vessel as there would be no cleats or points of attachment for any dock lines. Corey would have to toss them a lifeline and winch them aboard *Mariah*.

The woman on deck was bouncing up and down and screaming with excitement. Against the longest of odds, it appeared that they would be rescued by another boat, a boat that was almost certainly not a pirate vessel.

"Hello," Corey hollered above the sound of the wind and the waves. Corey wrapped a length of dock line around a winch and secured the line to a cleat on the port side of the transom. He tied a bowline to attach the lifesaving ring to the dock line. He raised the life ring in the air.

"If I toss this to you, can you catch it?"

"*Oui*, eh yes" the woman replied. "But *mon mari*, how you say, my husband is hurt."

"Secure the line to him first," Corey yelled. "I will winch him aboard and then throw the line back to you."

"*Merci, merci*" the woman replied. "Throw to me *s'il vous plaît*."

Corey threw the ring and attached line toward the woman, but it fell short. Corey retrieved the line and tossed it again, trying to compensate for the wind. After three tries he finally reached the woman, who impressively caught it in midair. She slipped the ring over the man, who appeared to be barely conscious, and secured it to him by clipping the rope encircling the life ring to the D-ring of his life jacket.

Once secured, she gave Corey a thumbs up sign and slipped her male companion off of the hull of the turtled cat and into the sea.

The seas had subsided considerably since the passing of the storm, and were now a relatively calm two to four feet. This was critical since the semi-conscious man was struggling to keep his head above water. Corey winched him slowly away from the stricken cat and toward *Mariah*, taking care not to submerge him in the process. He didn't want to drown the man while attempting to save him.

Once the man was alongside the bobbing yacht, Corey grabbed the line attached to the life ring with a boat hook, unwrapped the line from the winch, and pulled the man aft to the dive platform affixed to *Mariah*'s transom. Corey first checked the security of his tether before stepping over the transom and onto the dive platform. After securing his footing, he pulled the man onto the dive platform and then, using all of his strength and aided by an uplifting ocean swell, hoisted his dead weight over the transom and onto the aft deck where he landed with a thud.

Corey climbed back aboard *Mariah* and examined his passenger who was groggy and sputtering seawater, but alive. He detached the life ring from the life jacket and prepared to repeat the process with the woman waiting anxiously on the hull of the capsized sailboat. *Mariah* had drifted away while rescuing the man, so Corey steered the boat back alongside the hull of the catamaran.

"Are you ready?" Corey shouted.

"*Oui, oui s'il vous plaît*" was the reply.

Corey once again wrapped the line around the winch and tossed the ring toward the stranded woman. It landed short, but she dove headfirst into the sea and grabbed the ring. Corey began to winch her toward *Mariah*, but after covering half the distance to the boat she abandoned the ring, swam with clean powerful strokes to the dive platform and hoisted herself over the transom and onto the deck. Once aboard she took a moment to examine her semi-conscious companion and then wrapped her arms around Corey.

"*Merci, merci monsieur*, thank you *beaucoup* for saving us" she said through tears. "You are truly sent by the angels."

She knelt beside her husband and tried to revive him. Corey handed her a hydro flask filled with water filtered by *Mariah*'s reverse osmosis unit that captures rainwater, filters it and stores it for consumption. She drank thirstily and then turned her attention back to the man. Corey stowed the dock line and life ring in a starboard locker and returned to the cockpit to steer *Mariah* away from the floundering boat and into the wind. Once *Mariah*'s sails were unfurled and they were back on course under autopilot, Corey went aft to check on his unexpected passengers.

CHAPTER 11

Amelia

Corey knelt to examine the semi-conscious man. He peeled off his life vest and immediately noticed the injury. The man had been shot from behind through the left shoulder. There was an exit wound apparent, so at least the bullet was not lodged internally. Corey was a trained EMT. Although this wound would not be fatal under normal circumstances, it appears that the man had lost a lot of blood and there was a significant risk of infection. Corey was not equipped to manage such a wound aboard *Mariah*.

"What is his name?" Corey asked.

"He is JP, eh, Jean-Pierre. *Je m'appele* Amelia."

"What happened? Who shot him?"

"*Les pirates*. They chased us. Want me for slave, I'd rather be *morte*, eh, dead," Amelia replied.

"We motored. *Le vent,* the wind, was on our head. We pointed close into the wind to escape, but they were *très rapide.* We sailed *La Dolce Vita* into *la tempête,* into the storm. They did not follow. Shot at us. Jean-Pierre was shot" she said pointing to Jean-Pierre's wound. "But the storm was too strong for her. A wave *gigantesque* flipped her over" Amelia said, rotating her hands to emphasize the capsizing of their boat in the dangerous seas of the storm. "JP and me were thrown into the sea. Life vests saved us. I swam JP back to the boat. *Sans* food, *sans l'eau,* eh, water. *C'est un miracle* you found us. *Merci beaucoup, monsieur, merci beaucoup. Mon ange,* my angel" she said looking to the star-lit heavens above.

Corey and Amelia stripped the wet clothes from JP and partially wrapped him in a thermal emergency blanket. Corey retrieved *Mariah's* emergency medical kit and began dressing the wound. He inserted an IV line into a large vein evident on Jean-Pierre's forearm.

"Does Jean-Pierre have any allergies to drugs?" Corey asked.

"*Je ne se pas,* eh, don't know," she replied.

"Does he take any medications for heart problems or blood pressure?" Corey asked, pointing to his heart.

"No more, pills for *l'hypertension* sank."

Corey opted not to inject any form of penicillin given the lack of medical history and an unresponsive patient. He took out a vial of azithromycin and injected 500 mg into the IV fluid bag. He placed the IV bag into a portable battery-powered fluid infuser that enables the controlled delivery of fluids in emergency field circumstances, including the pitching deck of a sailboat in the middle of the Atlantic.

"Hopefully this will rehydrate JP and treat or prevent infection."

Amelia nodded, and clasped her hands as if in prayer. "*Les pirates*, I am afraid *monsieur* that they come back. Storm has passed. *Les pirates* want women very much."

"Please call me Corey. *Je comprends*, I understand," Corey replied.

"*Monsieur* Corey, *parlez-vous français?*" Amelia asked hopefully.

"Sorry, *Un petit peu seulement*, only a little," Corey replied.

Disappointed, but not surprised, Amelia shrugged. "*Mon anglais*, my English is not good."

"It is much better than my French I'm afraid," was Corey's reply. "Are you from France?"

"Non *Monsieur* Corey, from Quebec, Tadoussac, on *Le Fleuve Saint-Laurent*, the St. Lawrence river *en anglais*. Too cold there now," she said with arms wrapped around her in a simulated shiver. "Also *très dangereux*. JP and me, we sail to Bermuda before *le fleuve* freezes for winter. It is warm in Bermuda, and not so *fou*, how you say crazy. We hear this at least" she said.

Corey was instantly attracted to Amelia. She was beautiful, with long reddish-brown hair and the deepest blue eyes Corey had ever seen. In addition to her obvious physical beauty, Corey couldn't help but admire how strong this woman was, how calm she was in the face of so much recent trauma and the danger that they still faced.

The return of the pirates was a real concern. She was right, a beautiful woman like Amelia was a prize under any circumstances, especially for pirates who might not see another woman for months. They would certainly take her for themselves and then sell her to the highest bidder. Assuming they were able to outrun or otherwise escape the storm, they would be back for their prize.

"I too am sailing to Bermuda. We will turn off our lights at night," Corey said while switching off the cabin, running and masthead lights. "During the day we will keep careful watch on the radar for any ships in the vicinity. This is the best we can do."

"You have guns?" Amelia asked.

"Yes, I have a pistol for self-defense."

Amelia took Corey by the hand and looked into his eyes. "Promise me, *monsieur*, you shoot me before *les pirates* have me, *s'il vous plaît*. You must promise."

"I promise," Corey replied, although this was a promise he was not sure that he could keep.

Amelia released Corey's hand and turned to tend to JP.

Corey returned to the helm and prayed silently for their deliverance.

CHAPTER 12
Jean-Pierre

Day broke with another magnificent display of reds and oranges in the eastern sky. The air was crystal clear with only a few fluffy white cumulus clouds floating like pillowy balls of cotton dancing in a powder blue sky. The beauty of nature, the light blue of the sky blending into the deep navy blue of the sea flecked with white foam, always mesmerized Corey. He smiled as *Mariah* disturbed a school of flying fish that took to the air, sailing away from the leviathan that was *Mariah*'s hull. *I feel sorry for anyone who has never experienced this, which unfortunately includes most people,* Corey thought reflectively.

"*Il fait très beau,*" Corey heard a feminine voice behind him say. "Very beautiful."

Corey turned and looked at Amelia. *Yes, very beautiful indeed,* he thought. He instantly felt guilty for this thought and for his attraction to this woman. She was in a committed relationship with another man—a man who was his patient at the moment. He made a mental note to try and suppress his attraction to her, and not to reveal it to either her or to JP.

"How is JP?" Corey asked.

"He sleeps," Amelia replied. "But *je pense*, I think, is not well. Come see *s'il vous plaît*."

Corey and Amelia left the cockpit and entered the aft starboard cabin where JP was lying on a berth, covered with the thermal blanket.

"JP, are you awake?" Corey asked.

"*Oui*, eh, yes" was the reply.

At least he is able to respond now, Corey thought, *that's progress.* Corey noted that his color had improved, and his eyes appeared less sunken than when he was initially hauled on board.

"How do you feel?" Corey asked.

"Tired and cold" was the response. "I have been shivering and think I may have a fever."

JP's English is much better than Amelia's, Corey observed. "Let me check your vital signs."

Corey checked JP's pulse, which was thready and rapid, and opened his EMT medical kit. He took his temperature, which was 38° C, and checked his blood pressure, which was 110/60 mm Hg. "Your temperature is slightly elevated and your blood pressure is a little lower than I would like. You are probably dehydrated. Can you drink?"

JP nodded in the affirmative, "Yes please, I am thirsty."

Corey handed JP a bottle of flavored electrolyte solution. "In addition to this I think we should infuse another bag of IV solution and another dose of azithromycin. We need to get this infection under control."

After replacing the empty bag of IV solution in the portable fluid infuser, Corey changed the dressing on both the entrance and exit wounds where JP had been shot. Both wounds were obviously inflamed, especially the exit wound, which was more ragged and less clean than the entrance wound. Corey applied a topical antiseptic, and JP grimaced in pain.

"Are you hungry?" Corey asked.

"Not really" said JP weakly.

Amelia however nodded and said "*J'ai faim.*"

"We will prepare some food. You should try and eat something" Corey said to JP.

"OK," JP replied, nodding his head.

Corey lead Amelia to the galley and removed the storage container containing the mahi mahi from the onboard refrigerator. "Can you cook this fish please? I need to tend to something above-deck."

Amelia nodded, "*Oui, oui,* but of course" and began to make breakfast.

Corey left the cabin for the cockpit. He took out his binoculars and searched the horizon for any sign of another vessel. After assuring himself that they were safe for now, he opened one of the port lockers and removed the bosun's chair.

Corey attached the bosun's chair with a figure eight knot to the auxiliary halyard used to raise the mainsail in the event of power loss to the electronic sail furling mechanism. Corey planned to be hoisted in the bosun's chair to the masthead at the top of *Mariah*'s mast where he would remove the radar reflectors that had been permanently mounted there and had somehow survived the massive storm. This should make *Mariah* virtually undetectable to another vessel's radar and would increase their chances of avoiding detection should the pirates returned to search for *La Dolce Vita*. An accidental collision with another ship was much less of a concern than being captured by pirates.

Amelia's preparation of mahi mahi meuniere was delicious, and both Corey and Amelia ate heartily. Despite the rare feast of fresh fish that had been prepared, JP was only able to eat a few morsels. They left him to rest in the comfortable berth.

CHAPTER 13

The Crow's Nest

"Before we clean up after breakfast I need you to help me with something above deck," Corey said to Amelia.

"*Mais oui*, but of course" Amelia replied as she followed Corey out of the main cabin, into the cockpit, and onto the deck.

Corey lead Amelia to the base of the mast where he had left the bosun's chair attached to the halyard.

"I need you to use the winch and hoist me to the masthead," rotating his hand to simulate the cranking of the winch. "I need to remove the radar reflectors at the top of the mast."

"Ok, but is *dangereux*, no?"

"Not as *dangereux* as being detected by pirates" Corey replied. "It is fairly calm at present. I will furl the sails and turn the boat into the wind. We will use the motor to keep us into the wind. You will have to steer the boat and use this winch to hoist me to the masthead." Corey pointed to a winch mounted on the deck adjacent the helm. "Do you understand, eh, *comprenez-vous?*"

"*Je comprends*, I understand. I can do this, *pas de probleme*, how you say, no problem."

Corey gave Amelia a thumbs up and they both returned to the cockpit. Corey disengaged the robot autopilot, turned *Mariah* into the slightly breezy but pleasant wind blowing from the west southwest, and furled the sails. He handed the helm to Amelia and climbed onto the deck. After wrapping the halyard around the winch, he attached the winch handle to the self-tailing winch and proceeded to the base of the mast.

Despite the relatively calm wind and seas, *Mariah's* mast was swaying to and fro. *I've only done this in the harbor before,* Corey thought. *This is definitely not going to be fun.* Corey had heard horror stories of sailors who had fallen from the bosun's chair and plunged to their deaths or into the sea by having the halyard part or other equipment fail while attempting repairs in open water. *Mariah's* lines and equipment were sturdy and well maintained, but such accidents have happened, even when boats are docked in a protected harbor.

He secured himself into the bosun's chair, bit his lip, and gave Amelia the thumbs up to proceed. Corey used his hands to climb the mast as Amelia gently winched him skyward. He fought alternating waves of panic and vertigo as he ascended the mast and the pitching back and forth became more and more pronounced. Finally he reached the masthead where the dual radar reflectors were mounted. Trying not to look down, Corey removed the wire cutters from the pocket of his shorts. He carefully cut the strands of seizing wire that attached the reflectors to the stays at the masthead. After freeing the reflector mounted to the port side of the mast, he clipped the reflector to the halyard with a large carabiner and let it slide down the halyard to the winch where it landed with a loud thud. Amelia unclipped the reflector from the halyard and placed it on a cushion in the cockpit. Corey repeated the process to remove the reflector mounted to the starboard, and waited for Amelia to retrieve the second reflector from the halyard. Before descending from his temporary crow's nest, perched almost seventy feet above the sea, Corey took the opportunity to scan the horizon once more.

There, off the port bow, is that a boat? Yes, I think it is. Damn it. Headed north? Pirates? Can't be sure, but best to assume so.

Corey waved to Amelia to lower him from the masthead. He extracted himself from the bosun's chair, removed the halyard from the winch and cleated it off. Any relief he felt at being back on deck was overwhelmed by his alarm at the real and present danger posed by the vessel on the distant horizon. *At least they haven't detected us yet*, Corey thought, *or they would have changed course. Probably headed to where they assumed "La Dolce Vita" would have been if it had safely weathered the storm.*

Corey assumed the helm from Amelia, unfurled *Mariah*'s sails, and fell off the wind taking a course of 180°, due south—sailing a broad reach in the opposite direction to the course taken by the boat on the horizon. He cranked up the aqua-jet and began to motor sail at maximum speed. He needed to put as much distance as possible between *Mariah* and this other boat. Hopefully they had avoided detection, but the consequences were dire if they had not. *Best to hope for the best but prepare for the worst* as his dear mother had always said. *Sage advice*, Corey thought. He would take that advice now and flee.

CHAPTER 14

Precautions

Corey looked at Amelia with concern. Although he had only known her for a very short time, he had already developed a real affection for her. She was beautiful, smart, strong and gentle at the same time. *She cannot fall into the hands of pirate. We must take every precaution.*

"*Pourquoi*, eh, why do we change course?" Amelia asked. Her face showed concern, but not alarm, at least not yet.

"I saw a boat while at the masthead. Heading north. Could be pirates, I can't know for sure."

"They see us?"

"They did not change course, so we may be in the clear. But I think we need to take precautions and prepare just in case."

"We have guns, no?"

"We have only one pistol. Not enough to repel heavily armed pirates. We need another plan."

"We go fast yes, ten to fifteen knots?"

"They may be faster. I don't know what kind of boat it was, but it was moving very fast. If they catch us we need another plan, my pistol and flare gun will not be enough." *Think man think. What else can be used as a weapon?*

"Amelia, please stay in the cockpit and keep lookout. I need to go below and look for weapons." Corey climbed down the companionway steps into the cabin. He quickly checked on JP, and found him sleeping restlessly in his berth.

After checking on his patient, Corey looked around. *What can be used as a bomb, an explosive device?* Corey opened the lockers one by one, looking for anything that could be used as a weapon. In the forward locker on the port side of the boat inside an insulated container Corey found an array of lithium-ion batteries that were once connected to one of his solar units. *Wait, what about this? This can definitely explode. I thought I'd recycled these years ago.*

Corey remembered well how a lithium-ion battery can explode into flame. As an EMT in Sea Isle he had been called to the scene of a fire involving an electric vehicle that had been partially inundated by a king tide. After the tide had receded the owner attempted to start the car, but the sea water had penetrated, corroded and short-circuited the battery. Starting the vehicle triggered a chain reaction, violent fire and explosion that destroyed not only the car but the house as well. Although lithium-ion batteries had been largely replaced by sodium-ion batteries that are much more stable and much less reactive, Corey had forgotten to discard these. *This can definitely become a bomb, but how to deploy it? We can't very well throw it at them, and it will need to be in contact with sea water.*

Corey took the container with the batteries above deck into the cockpit and showed them to Amelia. "These can be made to explode, but we would need to find a way to deliver them to the pirate boat and expose them to sea water. I'm not sure how to do this yet, but let me think."

"*Peut être*, eh, maybe we won't need? Maybe they not come."

"Maybe, I just want to be prepared in case they do."

"I am *anxieux*, how you say, worried about JP."

"I am worried too. He has lost a lot of blood and I do not have any more IV bags of fluid. We need him to drink more of the electrolyte solution. Can you see if he will take some now?"

"*Mais oui*, but of course," said Amelia as she descended the stairs into the cabin.

How do we fashion a bomb out of these batteries? And how do we deliver it to the target? Corey thought while scanning the horizon for any evidence of unwanted visitors.

Amelia returned from the cabin. "JP, he is feeling stronger. He drank and ate a bar I took from *le galley*, *désolé*, eh sorry, is OK?"

"Yes, of course. It is important for him to regain his strength."

"JP, he is ready to come out soon *je pense*. The IV is no more. Can you remove please?"

Corey nodded his head and descended the companionway stairs into the cabin.

"Jean-Pierre, Amelia says that you are feeling better."

JP nodded, "I am still weak, but strong enough to leave the cabin and come on deck. I need to feel the wind in my face. Please remove the IV, I don't think I need it anymore" he said while extending his arm toward Corey.

"I hope that you do not need any more, since this was the last bag of solution that I have onboard." Corey removed the IV, placed a bandage at the puncture site, and helped JP out of the cabin and up the companionway stairs into the cockpit.

JP winced in pain as he sat down on a cushion next to Amelia. He put his arm around her and kissed her, then turned to face Corey. "Thank you again for rescuing us Corey. If it wasn't for you we would have either died on that boat, or been captured by the pirates. It truly is a miracle that you found us."

"Amelia, how did you know that I was sailing by, to send me that signal?"

"I, eh, see a light. *Peut être*, eh, maybe *une étoile*, how you say, a star, but it moves," as she pointed to the horizon. "I hear no engine, so maybe no pirate," shaking her head. "I take a *risque*, a chance. You Corey are *le miracle, une prière exaucée*."

"A miracle, an answered prayer," JP translated. "We are forever in your debt."

"If it was daytime, or if the moon was full or higher in the sky, I probably would not have seen the flashing light. We were fortunate indeed" Corey said and nodded toward Amelia. "But you, Amelia, were both strong and calm under these circumstances. Many would not have had the presence of mind to signal SOS with a flashlight. You, JP, have her to thank as well." JP nodded in agreement and kissed Amelia again.

Corey rose to his feet. "But we're not out of the woods yet, if you know this phrase. We are not safe. This afternoon Amelia hoisted me to the masthead in the bosun's chair. I saw a boat headed north at high speed. We have to assume that this is a pirate boat looking for *La Dolce Vita*. We have changed course, we are motor-sailing due south, but even if they find the wreckage of your boat, they may come looking for you, and their boat is much faster than *Mariah*," Corey said while patting her deck affectionately.

"We have only one pistol onboard. No other weapons other than these lithium iodide batteries, which can perhaps be fashioned into weapons, I'm just not sure how yet," Corey said, lifting them and extending his arm in JP's direction.

Corey pointed aft to the horizon. "There is no sign of them now, so perhaps I am being overly cautious. Let's discuss further over dinner. It's my turn to make *le dîner*. Please enjoy the late afternoon sun, the fair winds and the following sea as I prepare tonight's meal."

Corey descended the stairs and entered the galley. JP and Amelia held hands and kissed as they enjoyed the spectacular beauty of a late afternoon at sea.

CHAPTER 15

A Drone & The Green Flash

*M*ariah's crew of three sat on the cockpit cushions and enjoyed the last of Corey's dorado as another spectacular sunset was evolving to the west.

"We should enjoy this feast, as it's back to cold rations tomorrow I'm afraid," Corey said as he once more scanned the horizon to the north. "We don't dare slow down enough to try and catch more fish at this point. That would be too much of a *risque*, don't you agree *madame*," Corey said playfully to Amelia.

"*Oui monsieur*, no more *risques s'il vous plaît. La paix et tranquillité seulement*," Amelia replied.

"Yes, only peace and tranquility from now on please," echoed JP.

"But before we commit to peace, can we please take a moment to prepare for war?" Corey asked, while once again scanning the northern horizon. "Although there is no sign of unwelcome visitors at present, we should discuss how to deal with them should they find us.

We have one pistol. They will be heavily armed. *Mariah's* engines are solar and hydrogen fuel cell-propelled. Although hydrogen can be explosive, the fuel cell itself is designed not to explode. The only other possible weapon that I have on board are these lithium batteries," once more lifting them aloft. "They can be made to explode after contact with sea water, but there is no triggering mechanism and no way to deploy them."

"I have seen these types of batteries explode before, if you cut the insulation and throw them into the sea they may explode, but it is unpredictable. This does not seem to be a reliable weapon to me," said JP.

"JP was *militaire canadien*," Amelia offered.

"Yes, I served two tours of duty in the Canadian navy."

"Can you pilot an underwater drone?" Corey asked

"Yes, of course. Tethered or autonomous?"

"Autonomous, I use it to check on the integrity of structures, including *Mariah's* hull, after storms. It can tow fairly heavy payloads," Corey explained.

"We could theoretically cut the insulation on the batteries and tow them behind the drone to the other boat. Wrap them around a propeller so that even if the batteries did not explode, the propeller would be temporarily disabled."

"This might work JP. Are you skilled enough to do this?"

"I have not seen your drone, but I have a lot of experience operating such vehicles and am quite confident that this can be done. The target will have to be stationary of course, it will not work if the target vessel is underway and the propellers are spinning. Can I see your drone?"

"Let's finish dinner and I'll show it to you. We are moving too fast to do dishes, and I don't want to use fresh water since we don't know when it may rain again, so we will have to live with dirty dishes for a while I'm afraid," Corey shrugged.

After dinner Corey helped the stronger, but still visibly weak JP down the companionway stairs and through the cabin to the forward port side storage locker where the drone, or Autonomous Underwater Vehicle (AUV), was stored. Amelia remained in the cockpit to keep watch.

"This is a fully autonomous underwater vehicle," Corey explained. "The batteries are recharged automatically from the solar panel array on deck, so they should be fully charged now." Corey flipped on the on switch and confirmed that the battery was indeed fully charged. "The drone is controlled from this remote." Corey handed the remote to JP who nodded in understanding. "The drone is capable of full 360° freedom of movement underwater, and can also hover in place. These are 5000 lumen LED lights for illumination," Corey pointed to the dual light arrays in the nose of the AUV. "There is a 10K resolution high frame camera that also enables real-time viewing on the monitor in the remote control."

"Very nice. Can it tow a payload?" asked JP.

"Yes, it can tow a payload of up to five kg as long as there is no more than three knots of flow resistance from the current. Can you operate it?"

"Yes, although I have not operated this particular model, I have operated similar models from the same manufacturer before, and am comfortable with it."

"Hopefully this will not be necessary. But we can cut the insulation on the batteries and place them into this mesh bag." Corey removed a mesh bag from the locker and showed it to JP. "We can attach the mesh bag to this cable with a bowline. If we can get them to idle with some kind of diversion will you be able to wrap the cable around the propeller with the AUV?"

JP nodded his head. "I have done similar operations before while in the navy. Once the cable is in position, when they start their engine again it should wrap the cable around the prop. I'm assuming that their boat is propeller-driven and not jet-propelled. Otherwise obviously this may not work."

Corey nodded. "The pirates I have encountered fortunately do not have state-of-the-art technology. However, I agree, if they are jet-propelled we may have no way to escape, unless you have other suggestions?"

JP shook his head and grimaced. "We can try and use the same approach to blow up one of their jets, but it would be much harder to deliver the batteries and they would have to explode immediately. This will work much better with a more traditional propeller-driven boat. If it's a prop boat they will probably have two screws, either inboard or outboard. Shouldn't matter. Even if the batteries do not immediately discharge and explode, this should disable one of their engines making it difficult to maneuver and at the very least slow them down. To do this it would be best if I am in the cockpit so that I can have visual feedback on the location of the target as well as the image from the AUV. I probably should not turn on these powerful LED lights until I am aft of the target, so that they do not see the drone and start their engines."

Corey nodded in approval. "*Mariah* has two engines, a solar-powered dual aqua-jet and a hydrogen fuel cell-powered engine that uses the same jets, but delivers significantly more power. I had an earlier run-in with pirates and ended up using almost 90% of my hydrogen fuel cell battery capacity. There should be ten to fifteen percent left—enough for a brief burst that should allow us to quickly pull away from a disabled or partially disabled boat. They will shoot at us of course, so we would have to run everything on autopilot and lie flat on the deck once we decide to make a run for it. Are you well enough to do this? We don't want you to tear open your wounds by flinging yourself on the deck. We don't want you to lose any more blood."

"Hopefully this is just a thought experiment" replied JP. "But I don't see that I have any choice. Amelia cannot become a sex slave. I will die first," JP said with a determined look on his face. "What kind of diversion are you thinking of? We will have to get them to idle their engines for a few minutes to allow me time to operate the drone."

"I thought I'd raise the quarantine flag and tell them that we have the bird flu on board."

The avian flu had jumped to humans and become pandemic the decade before. The United States had not been prepared with an adequate supply of vaccines due to rampant vaccine hesitancy in the population and a government willing to manipulate science for political gain. Millions died as the mortality rate approached ten percent of those infected who were unvaccinated. The incidence and virulence of the virus diminished as more and more people developed at least partially immunity. However, avian H5N1 influenza, as with all flu strains, continually mutates and, as such, was still a serious disease. As a first responder, Corey was able to get the vaccine and had suffered only a mild bout of illness, whereas so many others who were not so fortunate suffered or died as a result. "You actually don't look well anyway my new friend, sorry."

JP shrugged and sighed. "Might work. Do you have a megaphone?"

"Yes." Corey opened a second locker and produced a megaphone. "I can talk to them using this."

"Sounds like a risky, but reasonable plan that with any luck we will never need to implement," replied JP.

Corey helped JP back up the stairs and into the cockpit where Amelia was keeping watch.

"*Bonsoir madame,* Looks like it will be a beautiful sunset" Corey observed.

"You have a plan?" asked Amelia.

"We have an emergency plan" offered JP. "If we meet any pirates you need to stay below while Corey and I execute the plan."

"We will give you the pistol. If it comes to a gunfight we will lose," Corey added.

"*Je me tirerais une balle,* I shoot myself then" Amelia replied looking first at JP and then Corey.

JP hugged Amelia. "We won't let that happen *mon amour.*"

Corey pointed west to the rapidly setting sun. *Time to change the mood.*

"Have you ever seen the green flash?" Corey asked his two passengers. "Tonight's sunset may be the perfect time."

"I have spent much time at sea, but have only seen the green flash a handful of times," JP replied as he gazed at the soon to be setting sun.

"What is the green flash?" asked Amelia.

"The green flash is caused by the refraction of light just as the sun sets below the horizon. The atmosphere acts like a prism. As the sun sets the prism refracts all wavelengths, the red light is absorbed, the blue light is scattered, and only a flash of green is seen," JP explained. "It can only be observed during ideal atmospheric conditions, usually when the air is warm and the sun sets over colder water."

"OK *mon professeur*" Amelia laughed. "Maybe *ce soir?*"

"Maybe tonight," both JP and Corey echoed.

They all gazed intermittently through sunglasses at the spectacular display of reds, oranges and purples as the sun dipped slowly but inexorably into the sea. Just as the last rays of the sun disappeared from the horizon there is was—the elusive green flash.

Corey, JP and Amelia simultaneously and spontaneously began to clap.

"Did you see it?" Corey asked

"*Oui, c'est fantastique,*" Amelia said excitedly.

JP nodded affirmatively. "Hopefully this is a good omen for safe passage to Bermuda." With that, JP began to rise. Amelia quickly stood to support him. "*Je suis fatigué*, I am tired. I need to go back to my berth."

Amelia helped JP to his berth and returned to the cockpit as the sunset continued its mesmerizing display of vibrant color.

"Can you please take the first watch tonight Amelia? I should also get some rest. Wake me if you see anything.

If not, I will relieve you at midnight and take the midnight watch. OK?"

Amelia nodded in affirmation. "*Oui oui mon capitaine*," as she saluted Corey in jest.

Corey fought back a sudden urge to kiss her, saluted back with a wink, and retired to the forward cabin for some well-earned rest.

CHAPTER 16

A Change of Course

Corey's alarm woke him at midnight and he groggily made his way into the galley to grab a can of synthetic coffee beverage. *Only a few left*, Corey noticed. *Hopefully JP is not a big coffee drinker.*

Corey staggered up the companionway stairs and into the cockpit where he found Amelia gazing at the dazzling night sky and the clearly visible Milky Way. "Quiet evening?" Corey asked.

"*Oui*, quiet *et beau. La mer, she* is beautiful *ce soir.*"

And so are you Corey said to himself.

JP you are one lucky guy.

"Are you tired?"

"*Un peu*, a little."

"Give me a few more minutes please, I need to use the head."

"*Pas de probleme*. I will be here."

Corey returned to the cockpit and relieved Amelia from her watch. "*Bonne nuit* Amelia. Sleep well."

Amelia responded, "*Merci* Corey. I will." as she descended the stairs and entered the aft starboard cabin to join JP in much-needed slumber.

The breeze had diminished somewhat and the seas had further calmed. *Mariah* was still making ten knots under sail, so Corey turned off the aqua-jet motor to preserve the battery. *Hopefully we are far from the pirate boat at this point and the rest of the journey will be like this. Calm beautiful weather, following seas, clear skies and pleasant company.*

Corey's graveyard shift was uneventful and pleasant. It appeared that they may in fact be out of danger, with no sign of pirates, just smooth sailing under clear skies and a waxing crescent moon. *This deviation has taken us off course. When Amelia relieves me, I need to do some calculations and replot our course to Bermuda. Maybe we can safely turn our running lights back on?*

Corey noticed the wind clocking around to the west northwest overnight. *Mariah*'s AI-enabled onboard computer had automatically adjusted sail position and *Mariah* was now essentially on a beam reach heading south. *This should be favorable winds for the next leg of the voyage, which will be more easterly,* Corey noted as the sun began to peak above the horizon to the east. *Despite the course modification we have to be within 100 nautical miles of Bermuda.*

"*Bonjour* Corey," Amelia greeted him from the companionway stairs, a can of synthetic coffee beverage in her hand. "I can watch now. *Temps de dormir*, time for sleep," she said while tilting her head to the side to rest on her clasped hands, a universal gesture for sleep.

The sun was just above the horizon. The dawn of what Corey hoped would be a peaceful and pleasant day at sea. "*Bonjour* Amelia. How is JP?"

"*Bien, merci*, he sleeps."

"Good, he needs to regain his strength. Before I rest I need to recalculate our course. We will miss Bermuda on our current tack."

"*Oui, je comprends*. OK, I take watch."

"*Merci*. I will be back shortly with our new course. *Madame*, you have the conn," Corey said with a playful expression.

Amelia looked at him with a puzzled expression. "*Quoi?*"

Corey laughed, "You are in charge."

Amelia stiffened into attention and looked at Corey with amusement. "*Mais oui monsieur*. Always."

"*Mais oui* indeed." They both laughed as Corey descended the stairs for another round of dead reckoning. He walked to the chart table and examined the nautical chart. *Mariah* was very stable, especially with following seas. Big cats like her are much less prone to heeling than a monohull, even when beating into the wind, making the cabin much more stable while under sail. Although Corey was not prone

to seasickness, he had lost his lunch on occasion while plot-
ting a course below decks in rough seas. Today fortunately
was not going to be one of those occasions.

Corey estimated that they had sailed for twenty hours at
an average speed of eleven knots against a current of approximately one knot. He marked on the chart the approximate
location where *Mariah* was on his previous rhumb line when
he saw the boat on the horizon and changed course. He took
out his drafting compass and marked a location 200 miles
due south of that position. He then took out his triangle
protractor and drew a straight line from the estimated current position, approximately 100 miles due east of Bermuda,
to his target, again taking currents and prevailing winds into
account. Corey returned to the cockpit and reset the autopilot course to 95°. *Mariah* gradually adjusted sail to her new
course, a downhill run toward Bermuda.

"New course plotted and assumed *mon capitain*," Corey
saluted as he spoke.

"*Je suis une femme*, I am a woman *monsieur, c'est **ma**
capitaine*," Amelia replied laughing.

"You are definitely a woman **ma** *capitaine, pardon-
ne-moi*," Corey said with a smile. Corey scanned the horizon
once more. *Nothing on the horizon* he noted with relief. "I will
now retire to my berth. Please wake me if anything changes."

"*Mais oui*, you can be sure," Amelia replied.

On his way down the companionway steps Corey prac-
tically ran over JP as he was working his way to the cockpit.

"JP, *bonjour*. Can I help you up the stairs. Can I get you anything?"

"*Bonjour* Corey. I would appreciate your support into the cockpit. If you would be so kind as to get me a bottle of the flavored electrolyte solution that would also be appreciated."

Corey helped JP up the stairs and seated him in the cockpit facing eastward so that he could enjoy the sunrise and feel the sun on his face. He retrieved a bottle of electrolyte solution and handed it to JP. *Glad he's not a coffee drinker, we can't run out of coffee,* Corey noted, and sauntered back to his berth to sleep leaving his two crewmates on watch above deck. *I need this sleep badly. I'm exhausted,* Corey thought as he quickly drifted off to sleep.

CHAPTER 17

Les Pirates

Three hours of peaceful slumber ended with a start. Amelia was shaking him vigorously. "Wake up, wake up *s'il te plaît. Les pirates, les pirates,*" she exclaimed as Corey finally responded to her not so gentle exhortations.

"What? What?" Corey mumbled groggily.

"*Un bateau*, a boat. He is coming."

Corey opened his eyes wide and sprang out of the berth. He followed Amelia into the cockpit, where she pointed at the boat quickly approaching from the northwest.

"Damn," Corey exclaimed. "I thought we'd lost them. There is no point in trying to outrun them now. JP, we must prepare to execute the contingency plan that we discussed yesterday."

JP nodded his head grimly in affirmation.

"*Quel est le plan?*" she said to JP, "What is the plan?" looking at Corey with panic in her eyes.

"JP and I have a plan to disable their boat. We have an underwater drone that JP will operate. We will wrap a cable around their propeller."

Corey put his hand in the air, index fingered raised. "Quiet please." Corey listened closely. He could hear the faint hum of a powerful engine. "Can you hear it? They have a traditional motor, maybe even fossil fuel-driven by the sound of it. This means our plan has a chance."

"But fossil fuels for marine purposes were outlawed 20 years ago. No modern boat would have such an engine," JP stated incredulously.

"They were outlawed in our countries, but not all countries followed suit. Many of the poorer countries in the Caribbean and to the south, all of which were heavily impacted by climate change, could not afford to make this transition. These are outlaws, and outlaws by definition will not abide by the law regardless of the country. My guess is that these pirates are from such a place. Amelia, you must go below now. They cannot see you or suspect that you are on board."

"*Où est le pistolet*, my gun, my gun" Amelia demanded. "I will not become slave."

"Go into the companionway now please, I will get the gun." Corey went below and returned with a 9mm handgun, which he handed to Amelia. "This pistol has eight rounds in the magazine. Do you know how to use it?"

"*Mais oui*," she said confidently.

"She knows how to handle a gun. She is a better shot than I am," JP offered in support.

Amelia descended the stairs into the cabin with Corey close behind.

"Great. Please don't kill yourself except as a last resort, when it is clear that all else has failed. If our plan works we will all survive."

"I am below, *comment je saurai*? How to know?"

"We will set the autopilot for maximum speed using the hydrogen fuel cell-propelled jet. Once JP has disabled their engine we will engage the autopilot and dive to the deck. *Mariah* will quickly speed away from their boat. They will try to follow, but, if the plan works, one of their screws will be disabled. At that point they will start shooting. JP and I will give you the all clear to come back topside when it's safe. If we fail and are either killed by the pirates or they board *Mariah* you will hear their voices and you can either surrender or end your life. It's really up to you."

Amelia looked at Corey with tears in her eyes. "You cannot fail Corey. You cannot fail."

Corey took Amelia by the hand and looked into her eyes. "We will succeed or die trying. That's all I can promise." Corey turned away from Amelia with a look of firm resolve etched into his face. He retrieved the quarantine flag, the lithium ion batteries and took them into the cockpit and handed the batteries and a knife to JP. "For the batteries."

JP shook his head, a look of grim determination on his face.

Corey looked again at the approaching boat, which now appeared to be about a mile away but closing fast. He went below again and retrieved the drone, the cable, and the mesh bag from the locker, placing them at JP's feet. They would have to slow *Mariah* significantly before dropping the drone over the side. Corey took the quarantine flag and raised it to the top of the mast using the auxiliary halyard.

The word "quarantine" is derived from the Italian word *quaranta*, meaning forty, which was the number of days that incoming ships needed to remain at anchor in the harbor before disembarking during the time of the plague. Forty days was sufficient to ensure that the incoming vessel did not carry the black death. Although the use of the term has broader applications today, the international maritime black and yellow quarantine flag is still recognized as indicating the presence of disease onboard ship. Corey hoped that its meaning would be well understood, even by pirates.

After raising the flag, Corey re-engaged the solar battery-powered aqua-jet, took *Mariah* off of autopilot and steered her into the wind to furl the sails. He programmed the autopilot robot to engage the hydrogen fuel cell-propelled jet engine at maximum acceleration and speed on voice command.

By the time Corey was finished, JP had scored the insulation on the batteries, placed them into the mesh bag and attached them and the trailing cable to the drone. They waited until the oncoming boat was within 300 meters before slowing *Mariah* and dropping the drone and its payload over the side.

The oncoming speedboat was a power catamaran. The roar of its engines subsided as they approached *Mariah*. Four large barrel-like containers were evident on the aft deck of the speedboat. *These must be spare fuel tanks*, Corey observed. *This is definitely an old-style fossil fuel-propelled power boat that has been modified for long-range cruising.*

The pirate boat pulled alongside *Mariah* and mirrored her speed, which Corey had reduced to three knots—the maximum speed that the AUV could maintain carrying a payload. JP sat in the cockpit, his back to the pirate boat, the remote control for the drone in his lap.

"JP, shooting at those fuel tanks could be an option if our plan doesn't work," Corey said quietly without taking his eyes off of the pirate vessel.

"I'm not sure that 9mm bullets will penetrate those tanks. Also, I'm not sure how we would get the gun from Amelia without either getting shot ourselves or letting them know that we have a woman on board. Of course, if this doesn't work, then we will have no choice but to shoot at them," JP replied.

Corey could see four men aboard the power boat—two in the cockpit and two on the foredeck. One man stood at the helm, the other three were pointing what appeared to be automatic rifles in Corey's direction. The boats were so close now that there was no need for a megaphone.

One of the men on the foredeck lowered his gun and shouted to Corey, "*Hola, parad vuestros motores.*"

Corey understood Spanish, they wanted him to stop the engine, but feigned ignorance. "*No habla.* I don't speak Spanish."

"Oh, English. It's OK, I speak. Stop your engines. We come aboard."

Corey needed to buy time for JP to perform the challenging and delicate maneuver of wrapping the cable around the propeller with the drone, which, in fact, would be easier when the engine is in neutral and the propellers are stationary and not rotating.

Corey cut his engine. The skipper of the pirate boat did the same. JP began his approach with the drone to the stern of the pirate boat. He did not turn on the bright LED lights until he had positioned the drone immediately astern. "I am in position, they have an inboard engine with twin screws. Buy me some time to wrap the cable around one of them."

Corey nodded his head indicating that he understood. He pointed to the quarantine flag. "We are flying a quarantine flag."

"What does it mean?"

"It means that we have sickness onboard. The bird flu."

"You don't look sick my friend," the man said with a slight chuckle.

"I took the vaccine. It is my brother here who is ill."

JP turned his head and weakly waved with a wan look on his face.

"Your *hermano* does not look well *señor*. Maybe we can help," he said with a wry laugh. "Although you do not look like *hermanos*, eh, brothers to me," the man chuckled again.

"We have different fathers, but the same mother," Corey replied.

"Make him stand," the man demanded.

"He is too weak from the flu," Corey replied.

"Why he not in bed then?"

"He gets seasick," Corey said, waving his head and hands side to side to mimic the rolling of the boat.

"I think you waste time. We took the vaccine also," the man said laughing. "We come onboard."

Apparently fear of a deadly disease was not going to be sufficient to deter these bastards, Corey thought grimly.

"It will be dangerous for you, very bad disease," Corey replied.

"It will be dangerous for you either way," the man said with a sneer on his face. "We can shoot you now, but we don't want to waste our bullets. Also, don't want to shoot the woman."

"There is no woman on board. It is bad luck to have women aboard a boat," Corey replied, raising his arms with palms up to feign deference.

"It *is* bad luck for you my friend," the man sneered. "I throw you a line, you winch us together. We search. If no woman we let you go," the man said with a grin.

Corey knew that this was a lie. The minute they were onboard they would slit their throats and throw them over the side. He looked at JP.

JP shook his head. "Almost, but not quite there yet," he said under his breath.

Corey looked at the man on the foredeck, now holding a dock line in his hand. The man threw the line to Corey, who intentionally missed it. The pirate retrieved the line and threw it once again in Corey's direction. Again, Corey clumsily missed the catch.

The other man on the foredeck and the one in the cockpit trained their rifles on Corey. The man with the dock line said, "You catch it this time or we will shoot."

Corey nodded that he understood. The man threw the rope and Corey caught it. "JP we are out of time."

"I think I have it," JP replied with a thumbs up sign that only Corey could see.

The men on the pirate boat lowered their weapons as Corey walked the rope to the winch located adjacent to, but just slightly to port of the helm. He pretended to wrap the rope around the winch. He looked at JP who nodded back. *Go time.*

Corey said, "engage autopilot," and the robot responded immediately. *Mariah*'s hydrogen fuel cell-propelled dual jet engine silently began to accelerate *Mariah* away from the power catamaran, leaving their dock line floating in the sea. Corey and JP dove head first onto the deck before the pirates understood what was happening. The two men with rifles raised their weapons to fire, but the man of the foredeck yelled to them, "No, you might hit the woman. We catch them. Move, *vámonos rápido*."

"Go baby go," Corey exhorted *Mariah* as she began to pull away from the still stationary power cat. Corey crossed his fingers and looked to the heavens in silent prayer. *This has to work, please make it work.* Corey raised his head to peek at the power boat now in *Mariah's* wake.

Corey crawled to JP who was still watching the monitor on the remote control of the AUV. He saw the propellers begin to rotate, but the starboard side screw quickly became entangled with the cable. The spinning propeller cut into the lithium batteries, enhancing the short circuit that JP had created with his knife. The batteries ignited and the intense heat generated quickly progressed into a thermal runaway reaction, starting a fire that water would not extinguish. The pirate ship rotated in a circle as only one propeller was providing thrust. Two crew members rushed to the stern to see what the problem was. They saw the starboard propeller with a cable wrapped around it. They shouted, "*Fuego, fuego,*" as they pointed at the white-hot fire that was now melting the propeller and threatening to damage the hull. "*Detener los motores, detener, detener,* stop!" The skipper stopped the engines and joined the other crew members at the stern as they watched the fire gradually creep into the hull. Their ship was disabled, potentially fatally. Now it was their turn to be in mortal danger.

One of the men picked up his rifle and began firing at *Mariah*, but she was quickly pulling away and the bullets fell harmlessly into the sea.

"*Ma chérie*, it worked, we are safe," JP called out to Amelia.

Corey and JP rose and hugged. "Congratulations my friend," Corey exclaimed.

"Brilliant plan, well executed." JP replied excitedly.

"Not so fast *hombres*," a dark voice said from aft. JP and Corey turned and looked at the man climbing over the transom, soaking wet, and pointing a pistol at them.

JP and Corey looked at each other in horror. *This man must have swum over while we were stalling for time and hauled himself onto the dive platform.* Corey realized. *Now what do we do?*

JP did not hesitate, he rushed the man who shot him twice. JP collapsed to the deck. Three shots rang out from the companionway stairs behind Corey's right shoulder, each striking the pirate center mass. The pirate fell backwards over the transom and into the sea.

Amelia dropped the pistol onto the deck and rushed to JP's body, now lying motionless on the deck. "*Non, non, non, non, mon amour. C'est impossible,*" she cried in anguish.

She looked at Corey with tears in her eyes, "*Aidez-moi* Corey, *aidez-moi. S'il vous plaît, s'il vous plaît,*" she cried to the heavens.

Corey rushed to JP's side and checked his vitals. He was not breathing and there was no pulse. He flipped JP over and examined the gunshot wounds—two to the chest, one directly over the heart. Corey choked back his tears. He tried to comfort Amelia, but she was inconsolable. They had escaped the pirates and exacted a heavy toll on them. But *Mariah's* crew had also paid a very high price. Jean-Pierre was dead and there was no way to bring him back.

CHAPTER 18

Funeral for a Friend

Corey stood at *Mariah*'s helm and stared blankly at the horizon, choking on his grief. Although he had only known JP for a few days, he had come to admire his new friend's strength and courage. *He was such a good man. Such a waste.* Corey didn't have many friends any more. It was beyond tragic to lose this one so quickly and in such a senseless manner. *He sacrificed himself for us. Bless you JP, may you forever rest in peace.*

Corey reached down and switched off the hydrogen fuel cell-propelled jet, there was only two percent showing on the battery. He activated the aqua-jet, steered *Mariah* into the wind, unfurled the sails and fell off to resume his previous heading of 95°.

He could hear Amelia wailfully crying below decks, which made Corey's grief all the more difficult to subdue. He hated to hear a woman cry, especially one that he had be-

CALL THE WIND MARIAH

come so fond of in such a short period of time. But there was nothing anyone could do, nothing he could say that would ease her broken heart.

JP's motionless body lay where it fell on the deck. He knew that they would have to bury him at sea, since the Bermudian authorities would not allow them to bring a corpse into their carefully curated country. He would discuss preparations with Amelia when she was ready. Corey covered JP with a thermal emergency blanket and returned to the helm. Although *Mariah* was once more on autopilot, Corey inexplicable felt better staring forward, scanning the horizon with his hands on the wheel.

A few minutes later Amelia appeared at the companionway door, still sobbing uncontrollably. Corey looked at Amelia with intense sorrow etched onto his face. *She is so beautiful, and so sad, I wish I could say something that would assuage her grief, even a little.* To his surprise, Amelia came to him and wrapped her arms around him. Although both were experiencing profound sadness, hers was much deeper and more intense. She had lost her spouse, her partner, the love of her life. Corey knew that she was not going to recover from this any time soon. He would try and comfort her as best he could.

Amelia looked at the body now covered with a blanket on the deck. "*Pourquoi? Pourqoui?* Why? How *l'homme, le pirate* get on board?"

"He must have swum over, perhaps underwater with a snorkel, and climbed onto the dive platform while we were buying time, stalling, with the other pirates. We needed time for JP to work the drone and disable the propeller." Both Corey and Amelia began to cry again at the mention of JP's name. Amelia hugged him and buried her face in his chest crying uncontrollably. For several minutes they both stood there in silence, lost in their thoughts and their grief.

"He was a very brave man, a true hero in every sense."

"*Oui*, he was a hero and much more *pour moi*," Amelia sobbed. "*Je suis perdue, je suis perdue,* I am lost."

Corey hugged her closer, wishing he could take some of her pain away, to absorb it somehow into his body, but only the tincture of time can offer some relief to this wound, a wound that will never truly heal.

Amelia gradually pulled herself together and sat on a cushion in the cockpit. "*Et maintenant*, what we do now?"

"We sail on to Bermuda as planned."

"*Et* JP? His *corps*, his body?"

"I am sorry, eh, *je suis désolé,*" Corey looked at Amelia with anguished eyes. "The presence of a body would raise many questions. We need to bury him at sea before we reach Bermuda."

Amelia looked at Corey again, tears streaming from her eyes. She shook her head. "*Je suis perdue.*"

"We have time, we don't have to do anything right now."

"*Il est parti*. JP is gone. *Son corps*, eh, his body, is not him. Maybe *ce soir*?"

Corey was a man blessed with, or some would say burdened with, an empathetic soul. When he looked at her he could actually feel her pain. "No need to decide now, I will plan for this evening, but if you want to wait it's OK."

"*Non, ce soir*, sunset," she said, shaking her head gently as she rose from her seat. As she walked past the helm to enter the companionway she touched Corey gently on the arm. He smiled at her. It was a sad smile just the same.

Corey set his grief aside and began to plan for a burial at sea. It was now late afternoon and sunset was only two hours away. *I don't know the protocol for burial at sea. Mom and Dad's ashes were scattered in the ocean, but this is very different. We will need to weigh the body down to keep it on the sea floor, we don't want it floating to the surface. I have a spare anchor in the anchor locker on the foredeck. That should do the trick.*

Corey climbed out of the cockpit, skirted around the mast and onto the foredeck inside the fully unfurled jib. He opened the anchor locker and removed the spare anchor, anchor chain and anchor line from the locker. *I'll have to shorten the anchor line, it's too long for this purpose.* Corey removed his rigging knife from his pocket and cut the line approximately two meters from the shackle that connects the chain to the nylon anchor line. He carried the anchor, chain and shortened rope across the deck and back into the cockpit. Next, he tied a section of the rope around JP's bare feet using an anchor hitch knot, leaving a length of line long enough to extend from the anchor hitch knot to the belt of JP's shorts where he tied a clove hitch. He left some play in the line so that the length of line secured to the belt would only be needed if the anchor hitch on the feet were to slip off.

Very grim duty, Corey thought, wiping tears from his eyes. *So sorry my friend, so very sorry.*

Finally, he went below and retrieved a spare bedsheet, which he wrapped around the body and tied it in place with sections of braided polyester rope. He carried the anchor and then JP's shrouded body to the edge of the transom on the afterdeck. He would place the anchor and JP's body, perhaps with Amelia's help if she was so inclined, onto the dive platform before committing him to the sea.

Corey looked up and saw Amelia exiting the companionway door. "I have prepared him for burial at sea as best I can."

Amelia looked at the body of her husband covered in a makeshift shroud. She shook her head and turned away teary-eyed. "I have seen *beaucoup de mort,* so much death *dans ma vie.* So many *disparu.* Some say *la mort apporte la paix,* death brings peace," as she turned her head to face Corey once more. She pointed to her heart and said "I pray Jean-Pierre has peace now," in her halting English.

Corey looked at Amelia's face marked with sadness, and he felt his heart begin to break. "I too have seen so much death, so many loved ones who have perished from senseless violence or preventable disease. It does not make the loss of someone you love any easier to bear. I am deeply sorry for the loss of Jean-Pierre. I did not know him long, but he was a man of great courage, great valor. If any man deserves to rest in peace it is this man," he said as he pointed at the body lying next to him.

Corey and Amelia both looked at the horizon. The sun was just beginning its glorious descent once more into the sea.

"*Il est temps je pense. Il est temps,*" Amelia said as she looked down at her bare feet on the deck.

"Yes, it is time. I will take *Mariah* off of autopilot and shorten sail, *un moment s'il vous plaît.*" Corey quietly walked to the helm and slowed *Mariah* to approximately three knots. "Is there something that you'd like to say?"

"*Au revoir mon amour, à bientôt au paradis Jean-Pierre, mon héros.*"

Amelia went to Corey's side and together they hoisted first the anchor and then JP's body over the transom and onto the dive platform. Corey climbed over the transom and onto the platform next to JP's body. He looked at Amelia who nodded tearfully for Corey to proceed. Corey looked to the heavens and said "We commend the soul of this righteous man to you as we now commit his body to the sea." With that Corey slipped the anchor off the dive platform, followed by the shrouded corpse of Jean-Pierre. They both watched as the body disappeared under the waves. Corey saluted his departed comrade. "*Au revoir* my friend. We will see you on the other side."

Corey climbed back over the transom trying to hold back his emotions. Amelia wiped the tears from her eyes, gave Corey a brief hug, and descended the companionway stairs into the cabin.

Corey watched as the sun set in the west and the moon began to rise in the east. He had just buried a near stranger at sea, but he felt a burden of sadness and guilt incommensurate with the short duration of the intersection of his life with that of Jean-Pierre. *This man saved my life and Amelia's life. How can I ever repay him? I promise to deliver his wife safely to Bermuda or forfeit my life in the process. It is the only thing I can offer in return.*

With that Corey reset the autopilot, unfurled the sails and resumed course for Bermuda. There would be no green flash tonight, or perhaps ever again.

CHAPTER 19

Bermuda Beckons

The crescent moon was high overhead as midnight approached. The winds had died substantially after sunset and *Mariah* had slowed to approximately five knots under full sail in calm seas. Her running lights and masthead light were still switched off, making the stars, the moon, and the glow from the bioluminescent dinoflagellate zooplankton in *Mariah*'s bow wave and wake the only light visible. The night was peaceful, serene, almost ethereal, a welcome contrast to the turbulence and violence of the day.

Corey remained ever vigilant despite his grief. Although he and JP had almost certainly disabled and probably sank the pirate boat that had been stalking them, there were likely many other sea-faring predators hunting for prey in the North Atlantic Ocean. He was mentally prepared to remain on watch all night to allow Amelia to sleep. To his surprise

Amelia appeared slightly after midnight to join him in the cockpit.

"*Je ne peux pas dormir,*" she said softly, "Sorry, can't sleep."

Corey looked at Amelia with sympathy. "Perhaps some fresh air will help you fall asleep. I may have some beer in the refrigerator if that would help."

"*Non, merci.* I stay awake. Take my watch. *C'est à moi,* my turn," she replied pointing to her chest.

"Would you like some company?"

"*Non merci,* I need to be alone, *maintenant,* eh, now."

"OK, I will try and get some sleep. I will relieve you at 4:00. We should be entering Bermudian waters late tomorrow. I suggest we spend some time preparing *Mariah* and ourselves for the Bermudian authorities. OK?"

"*Mais oui, parfait,* perfect," Amelia replied, although her face showed that things were far from perfect.

Corey descended the companionway stairs, leaving Amelia alone with her sorrow. Despite the exceptional beauty and calm of this peaceful night at sea, Amelia felt no relief from the deep emotional pain and emptiness that now consumed her. Tears flowed from her eyes as she searched the heavens for answers. "*Pourquoi? Pourquoi?* Why? Why?" But the only reply was the sound of the wind and the waves, a slight luffing of the sails, and the clanging of the stays against the mast as *Mariah* skimmed almost effortlessly across the surface of the sea.

The alarm startled Corey awake at 4:00 am. It had been a restless three and a half hours of sleep, but it would have to do. *There will be plenty of time to rest after making landfall,* Corey thought with a half-smile on his face. *Unless I have miscalculated, we should be in Bermudian territorial waters by nightfall.*

After grabbing a synthetic coffee beverage from the re-frigerator, Corey climbed the companionway stairs and en-tered the cockpit where he found Amelia staring blankly at the horizon. He could almost feel her pain welling up in him. "Hello Amelia. I can take over now. Please try and get some rest."

Corey's voice interrupted Amelia's trance-like reverie. She looked at Corey with a grim smile and replied, "OK, I try to sleep now," as she left the cockpit for her berth below deck.

Corey shook his head in sorrow as he watched her de-scend the stairs. *It will take a long time for her to recover from this. I will comfort her as best I can, but I'm not sure there is anything I can do or say that will ease her pain.* He spent the next few hours standing at the helm or seated in the cockpit, intermittently scanning the horizon as he waited for the sun-rise, lost in his own thoughts.

As daybreak approached, Corey's thoughts turned to preparing for the final phase of the journey. *After sunrise we will take some time to make Mariah shipshape before we en-counter any Bermudian coast guard or navy vessels. It will do both of us good to get our minds off of JP and onto something constructive.*

The sun was already well above the horizon before Amelia returned from below deck. Corey had just opened the hatch to the aft deck storage compartment and uncoiled the salt water hose. He looked up from hosing and swabbing down the deck as Amelia entered the cockpit. "*Bonjour* Amelia. Did you finally get some sleep?"

"*Oui, un peu. J'étais très fatigué.* Sorry, I was very tired. I will try more English now, less *français*," she said with a determined look on her face.

"It's OK, I understand more French than I speak," Corey replied.

"Bermuda is English, yes?"

"Yes, Bermuda is English."

"Then help me with English, *s'il te plaît.*"

"*Mais oui*, Corey replied. I will."

"What can I do? *Pour aider*, eh, to help I mean."

"Please straighten up in the cabin and, especially the galley. We will furl the sails and drift for a while so we can wash both the dishes and ourselves. It has not rained in days, so we will need to clean the dishes and ourselves in salt water. We can however treat ourselves to a fresh water rinse, at least for our hair." He smiled, "we don't want to look like pirates when we meet the Bermudian authorities."

Amelia half-smiled back and nodded before disappearing once more below deck. After washing the dishes in the salt water sink, she returned with the dishes housed in a mesh dive bag. She tied the bag to a dock line with a bowline, cleated the line to *Mariah*'s stern, and heaved the bag over the transom to be rinsed. Corey smiled at her, *I guess the technique for washing dishes on a sailboat transcends borders.*

After Corey and Amelia had cleaned *Mariah* from stem to stern, Corey turned her into the wind, and furled the sails. The seas and the wind were calm—not ideal conditions for sailing, but perfect conditions for a swim. *Mariah* bobbed gently in the waves and drifted slowly in the weak current.

Corey and Amelia stripped down to their bathing suits. Corey tied a life preserver to a six-meter line cleated to the stern, grabbed the bottle of Joy dishwashing soap and dove off of the transom with Amelia right behind.

Swimming in the deep blue ocean was somehow less terrifying with company. In fact, the dip seemed to be a tonic for Amelia's spirits and she managed a smile in Corey's direction. They both hoisted themselves onto the dive platform, lathered their bodies with Joy dishwashing detergent, especially their hair, and dove back into the sea to rinse. Corey couldn't help but admire Amelia's slender, lithe form and graceful movements. *She is truly a remarkable woman, strong, athletic, alluring.* Corey returned to the dive platform and offered his hand to Amelia. She took his hand and he gently pulled her back onto the boat. Her touch was electric. He was falling hard. She offered a perfunctory smile, grabbed a towel and disappeared again down the companionway stairs for a freshwater rinse in the shower situated in the aft starboard head.

Corey felt a pang of guilt. *JP died yesterday saving our lives and I'm already falling for his widow. What is wrong with me?* he thought, shaking his head in disgust. *Who am I kidding, I fell for her the minute she climbed aboard.* He retrieved and stowed the life preserver and the deck line, and returned to the helm to resume course.

Corey looked to the west. The wind gods were apparently taking a breather as there was now only a slight breeze from the west northwest. Corey unfurled the sails, but headway was slow. He contemplated turning on the aqua-jet, but reconsidered. *Might be better to approach landfall in daylight. Limping along under full sail at five knots or less might be the best at this point. Don't want to run aground with no GPS and no local knowledge. Tomorrow will be here soon enough.* He set the autopilot and waited for Amelia to return.

"We are going to slow sail overnight and make landfall in the daylight."

"*Bonne idée,*" she hesitated, *Non,* English, good idea, safer."

Corey nodded in agreement and headed below for a freshwater rinse of his own.

Amelia watched as Corey disappeared below deck. She stared into space wondering what the future might hold for her now that JP was gone. *Je ne sais pas quoi faire maintenant.* "I don't know what to do now," she said aloud, shaking her head slowly in sadness. "*Je ne sais pas.*" She felt herself welling up again with emotion and wiped the tears from her eyes.

Corey reappeared, freshly rinsed and freshly shaven.

Amelia looked up from her state of hazy reflection. "*Tu t'es rasé*, you shaved."

Corey could see that she had been crying. It hurt him to see her so unhappy. "Yes, we should make contact with the Bermudian authorities sometime tomorrow, unless my navigation is off. I want to look as clean-cut as possible. They are very selective as to who they will accept into their island nation. Most are turned away, and in some cases forcibly repelled. But I have a sister in Hamilton."

"*La capitale.*"

"*Oui,* the capital. I have not been able to speak to her in over two years, but I have to assume that she is still there and still safe. She is a surgeon, a very talented woman, so she and her husband, who is also a doctor, are valuable members of the community. I am counting on her being my, I mean our, ticket in."

"What about me?"

"I've been meaning to speak with you about this, but I've been waiting for the proper time. You are grieving, and I don't want to suggest anything that would make you uncomfortable."

Amelia looked at him with a puzzled look on her face. "What will make me more *inconfortable?*"

"You don't know me of course, we have been thrown together by circumstance, but I would like you to trust me."

"I know you only a little, *mais* you seem *vrai,* eh, genuine. *Je n'ai vraiment pas le choix,*" she said, shaking her head. "Do I have choice? *Non,* I think not. I must trust you."

"Do you have a passport?"

"*Non, mon passeport* he sank with *La Dolce Vita.*" *Je n'ai pas d'identité,* she realized with a start. "I have no identity," she said with a look of panic on her face. "What do I do?"

"I assumed as much. This is what I suggest, and please do not take this the wrong way. I will tell the authorities that you are my wife, and that you lost your passport in a flood."

Amelia at first was taken aback. She looked at Corey with an expression of surprise and bewilderment. Then her expression changed to one of understanding. "*Merci* Corey, *merci.* You save me once again." With that she arose from her seat and to Corey's surprise gave him a hug.

"Do you have a wedding ring? I noticed that you and JP did not wear rings."

"*Les Québécois,* the Quebec people, often do not marry. We live together, we love, we have *les enfants,* but *pas de mariage traditionnel, pas d'église,* no church, no wedding, no *changement de nam,* eh, no change to name."

"Why is that?" Corey asked.

"*La révolution tranquille,* the quiet revolution. Against *l'église,* against the power of the church."

Corey didn't fully understand, but nodded his head as if he did. "I was engaged once, we loved each other very much. We were planning a wedding, but American society collapsed, descended into chaos and violence. I bought wedding rings in anticipation, but we never married. I still have the rings."

Amelia looked at Corey with sympathy. "I am sorry." She then shook her head in concurrence. "Things were bad also in Canada. *Le changement climatique*, the climate changed, *l' environnement* collapsed, *météo imprévisible*, the weather unpredictable. Very bad, very hot summer, very cold winter. *La pluie*, eh, the rain *torrentielle, l' inondation* - the flooding. *Très dangereux*. Very bad. So we bought *La Dolce Vita* and left." Tears once again appeared in her eyes and she looked away, remembering the tragedies that had befallen her and her de facto spouse.

"Things are *très dangereux* everywhere I'm afraid. Bermuda is supposed to be safe. We can both start new lives there, but first we have to get in. And that may be the tricky part. I need to somehow reach my sister, and she will need to vouch for us, to support our entry if you understand. Perhaps if we wear wedding rings it will be more convincing?"

Amelia shook her head in affirmation. "OK. *Je comprends*. I will wear the ring. I will pretend. I understand."

"OK, then it is settled. We will put the rings on tomorrow morning. I will do most of the talking with the authorities. OK?"

"*Mais oui*, of course." She smiled at him and then looked away. The sun was just about to set in majestic shades of red and purple. *Ciel rouge le soir, laisse bon espoir; Ciel rouge le matin, pluie en chemin.*

"Red at night, sailors delight," Corey offered aloud.

Amelia looked at Corey and laughed. "This is what I was just thinking now."

"Do they also say this in Quebec?"

"They say this everywhere, everywhere there are sailors, *je pense*" Amelia replied with a smile.

As the sun sank into the sea Corey noticed a shape just above the horizon. It was something that he hadn't seen since leaving Sea Isle—a bird. Sea bird populations had plummeted worldwide as their nesting sites, including entire islands, were inundated by the rising tides. Many species became extinct.

"Look Amelia, a sea bird!" Corey exclaimed.

"*Fantastique*, what kind?"

Corey went below and grabbed his binoculars from the shelf above the navigation table in the main cabin. The bird was now closer to *Mariah* and Corey was able to get an excellent view as it danced above the waves backlit by the setting sun. "It appears to be a petrel of some sort."

"*Magnifique*, rare bird."

Corey studied the form gliding along the tops of the waves as it passed behind *Mariah*, no longer backlit by the sun. "I think this is a Bermuda petrel, the national bird of

Bermuda" Corey said excitedly. "A rare bird indeed! The Bermuda petrel is a ground-nesting bird that was saved from extinction by conservation efforts earlier this century. Apparently their efforts continued even during this global catastrophe. Amazing!"

Amelia looked at Corey with surprise. "*Pourquoi* you know so much about birds?"

"My dad was a bird watcher. In fact, he was a marine naturalist, knew everything you ever wanted to know about marine life and more. My love of the sea is his legacy. He passed it on to me. I miss him every day." Corey looked away. Even after a decade the memory of his lost parents, their lives tragically cut short by a mindless, heartless, soulless drone, still brought tears to his eyes.

Amelia stood and gave Corey a hug. Tears filled her eyes. "We have both lost much it seems."

Corey hugged her back, feeling emotion welling up in him. She pulled away and looked once more at the setting sun.

"Perhaps we see the green flash *ce soir, non?*"

"Perhaps." Corey replied. *But it is hard to see the green flash when your eyes are full of tears,* he thought sadly.

"This bird, he is a good omen?" Amelia said, her eyes still focused on the last rays of the setting sun hoping for the green flash.

"He is a good omen indeed," Corey replied as the sun disappeared below the horizon without the elusive green flash. "Tomorrow is a big day. Let's get some rest. I'm exhausted. I'm sure that you are as well."

Amelia nodded in agreement.

"Shall you take the first watch, or shall I?"

"I take the midnight shift *cette nuit*, eh, tonight. OK?"

"Of course. Have a good sleep then. See you around midnight."

Corey watched as Amelia descended the companionway stairs, admiring her from behind. *She is such an incredible woman. If I could bring JP back I would. But I hope that she will eventually love me the way I'm starting to love her.*

Corey stared at the still tranquil sea and dreamed of a better life to come.

CHAPTER 20

An Omen

Amelia relieved Corey shortly after midnight. The night was still and the stars were bright in a cloudless sky. Corey pointed to the masthead light. "I turned our running lights back on. If we were to encounter the Bermudian coast guard or navy at night I don't want them to think that we have any reason to hide, or are engaged in any criminal activity."

"*Bonne idée*," Amelia replied, wiping the sleep from her eyes as she sat next to Corey in the cockpit. "Hopefully *les pirates* are dead, at the bottom of the sea."

Corey shook his head. "That is where they belong. In hell." He arose, nodded at Amelia and descended below deck for his turn at slumber.

Amelia continued to scan the horizon but there was nothing to see but the moon, the stars and the occasional flying fish startled by the bow wave. Occasionally she saw what appeared to be shapes moving in the distance above the horizon. *L' oiseau peut-être.* "Birds?" she said with a shrug. But the shapes were never close enough to know whether they were in fact birds or just her imagination.

Corey returned slightly after 4:00 with a coffee drink in his hand. "*Bonjour* Amelia. Would you like a coffee?"

"*Non, merci.* I will sleep more please."

"OK, *bonne nuit*," Corey offered as he exchanged places with Amelia in the cockpit. "Today is the day we make contact with Bermuda. I am confident."

"I hope we are welcome. *Non*, I pray we are welcome," she replied glancing up at the heavens briefly, before turning and making her way down the stairs into the cabin.

It was almost daybreak when the winds began to freshen. *Mariah* began to pick up speed and was once more cruising at almost ten knots. Corey smiled as he enjoyed the renewed motion of his speedy catamaran skipping through the waves and skimming over the surface of the ocean.

Shortly after daybreak Corey noticed what appeared to be shapes in the water dancing in front of the boat. He donned a life jacket, secured a tether to his jacket, and made his way to the foredeck. To his amazement he saw a pod of dolphins riding the pressure wave generated by *Mariah*'s bow as she sped through the water. The agile mammals danced to and fro, cutting back and forth through the wave as if riding the surf. As Corey looked around he realized with astonishment that there were not just a few individuals speedily coursing through the water off *Mariah*'s bow, but there were literally hundreds of dolphins, a mega-pod, swimming effortlessly before and beside the boat, easily matching and even surpassing *Mariah*'s speed.

I have to wake Amelia. She must see this, this is amazing, Corey thought as he made his way back into the cockpit and below deck to Amelia's berth.

"Amelia, Amelia, wake up please," Corey exclaimed with excitement as he shook her gently.

Amelia woke with a start. "Pirates?" she said with a look of alarm.

"No pirates. Dolphins, hundreds of dolphins. Please come see. It's incredible."

Amelia followed Corey above deck where Corey handed her a life preserver and a tether so she could join him on the foredeck. Even from the cockpit they could both see the stampede involving hundreds of animals swimming and leaping around the boat. The surface of the sea was alive with lithe torpedo-shaped bodies. Corey and Amelia made their way to the foredeck to watch the acrobatic display of these sleek agile creatures surfing *Mariah*'s bow wave.

"*Incroyable! Fantastique!*" Amelia was overwhelmed with excitement and was literally jumping up and down like a young girl. "I have never seen such a sight. In Tadoussac we have many whales. Many belugas, but not so many as this!"

Corey smiled at her. *She is so full of life, so much joie de vivre.* "In New Jersey we primarily have bottle-nosed dolphins. We would see them often in small pods or individually, but never like this. These must be common dolphins. Common dolphins are known to form these types of mega-pods, called stampedes when they move like this, rapidly and in synchrony. I have seen this on television, but never in person. It is truly incredible!"

Scattered throughout and above the surging mega-pod were scores of sea gulls. *Laughing gulls, ring-billed gulls, we must be close to land,* Corey thought with a smile.

Amelia looked at Corey and smiled. "This is a *bon présage,* a good omen. We must be near Bermuda, *non?*"

"These common dolphins can be found far offshore, but in these numbers and in the presence of so many sea gulls, there must be a large food source here. Perhaps we are closing in on or are even sailing above the Bermuda Pedestal."

Amelia looked curiously at Corey. "Bermuda Pedestal?"

"The Bermuda Pedestal is a seamount or underwater mountain—the remnants of an extinct volcano—the peaks of which form the modern islands of Bermuda. So yes, this is indeed a *bon présage,* a good omen."

Amelia looked at Corey with excitement. "Today we find a new home, I am sure."

Corey looked at Amelia and smiled. He was not as confident as Amelia as to how they would be received. But he didn't let on. "Today is a fresh start for both of us, for sure."

They climbed back into the cockpit as the stampeding dolphins began to disperse, leaving *Mariah* for other pursuits.

Amelia offered to prepare breakfast from Corey's dwindling provisions, leaving Corey alone in the cockpit lost in thought. The promise of Bermuda appeared to be close at hand. Would it be a warm reception? Or a cold slap in the face? It appears that he would soon learn the long-awaited answer to this critical question.

CHAPTER 21

Blessing of the Rings

After enjoying a light breakfast in the cockpit with Amelia and quickly cleaning up the galley, Corey went to his cabin and returned with the box housing the pair of wedding rings that he had purchased for his then fiancé what now seems like a lifetime ago.

Corey opened the box and showed the contents to Amelia. "These are the rings that we discussed yesterday. We should probably put them on now so that we don't forget."

Amelia stood across from Corey and looked at the two gold rings sitting side by side, gleaming in the morning sun. "*Très beau* Corey, beautiful rings. I am sad for the situation, *mais*, will wear it *avec plaisir*, eh, with pleasure."

Better to hand her the ring than to slide it on her finger. Don't want this to be any more awkward than it has to be. With that thought, Corey removed the smaller of the two rings and handed it to Amelia, who accepted the ring and slid it on the ring finger of her left hand.

"Does it fit?" Corey asked.

"*Oui,* as if she was made for me," Amelia replied, as she extended her hand and spread her fingers to admire the ring now sparkling against her sun-kissed skin.

Corey smiled at her. To his relief she smiled back. He slid the man's ring onto his finger and, like Amelia, admired the shining gold band now adorning his ring finger. "We will not have any tan lines on our fingers. Hopefully no one will notice."

Amelia nodded, "We can explain. *Pas de problème.*"

"No problem," Corey agreed. "We should probably decide on a story as to how we met and how long we have been married."

Amelia nodded in agreement. "OK, makes sense."

"I spoke to my sister just over two years ago, and did not say anything about a new girlfriend. Let's say that we met when your boat sank near Sea Isle last year and I was one of the first responders who came to your rescue. We fell in love and married shortly thereafter, so married about a year."

"OK, sounds possible, and with some truth." Amelia said, nodding again.

Don't want to read anything into that, her English is not perfect. Corey smiled at her none the less.

"You were fleeing dangerous conditions in Canada. We both decided to leave the U.S. because it was becoming too dangerous there as well. The rest of the story, the storms, the pirates, is real." *Should I tell her not to mention JP, or just assume that she will know not to? I don't want to make her cry.*

"I will not say about losing JP to *les pirates*. Best to keep secret, yes?" Amelia said as if reading Corey's mind.

Corey looked at her and shook his head sadly. "Probably best to keep this between us. Will confuse our story and may cause suspicion with the authorities. Sorry, we will have to keep his memory in our hearts alone, at least for now."

"*Je comprends*. I understand," as she looked away from Corey and stared at the horizon to conceal the pain once more welling up inside her.

Corey put his hand gently on her shoulder. "He was a great man, a hero. We will honor his memory by surviving this journey and finding new homes in a safe place, which was his dream as well as mine."

Amelia looked at Corey through teary eyes. "He was hero, *absolument*. I will never forget the sacrifice. But I will be strong," she said with conviction.

Corey looked at her with admiring eyes. "You are perhaps the strongest woman I have ever met. I know that you will be."

Amelia wiped away her tears, looked Corey in the eyes, and nodded her head. "I will be." With that she turned away and left the cockpit, descending the companionway stairs once more to return to her cabin below.

CHAPTER 22

Interdiction

Corey scanned the horizon for signs of land or of any ships or boats. Sea gulls were now frequently visible. *We have to be close. I'm surprised that we have not made landfall or at the very least made contact with the coast guard or navy. My navigation cannot be that far off.*

There in the distance he saw what appeared to be a glint of sunlight and a small object well off the starboard bow. Corey trained his binoculars on the object. *Looks like a boat, but can't be sure. We do not have radar reflectors any more, perhaps that's why we have not yet been detected?* Corey went below and checked the masthead radar. There on the display was an unmistakable blip off the starboard bow, with a signature typical of a ship.

"Amelia, it appears that we have company," Corey called out.

Amelia immediately appeared at the door to her cabin. *"Garde côtière Bermudienne, ou les pirates?"* she asked with alarm.

"We should be in Bermudian waters. It appears to be a large vessel closing at high speed. I think it more likely to be coast guard or navy, but please have the pistol handy just in case."

Amelia retrieved the pistol and both she and Corey climbed out of the cabin and into the cockpit. Amelia placed the pistol under a cockpit cushion and waited with Corey for the arrival of the large boat now closing on their position. Corey looked at the masthead and realized that the quarantine flag was still flying. "Damn, I never took down that flag," he said to Amelia, pointing to the black and yellow flag flying from *Mariah's* mast. Corey scrambled to the base of the mast and quickly lowered the flag, hoping that the approaching boat was too far away to notice. He returned to the cockpit and stowed the flag below decks, grabbing his megaphone in the process.

The approaching vessel was now close enough for Corey to make out her markings with the binoculars. She was indeed the Bermudian coast guard, proudly flying the British red ensign with the Bermuda coat of arms. Although Bermuda declared independence from the United Kingdom in 2047 and closed her borders after an influx of immigrants fleeing environmental catastrophe in the mother country, she never changed her flag or her affection for the Crown. As a consequence of independence, Bermuda was responsible for her own defense and had established her own coast guard and navy including two large cutters, two destroyers and three naval frigates patrolling her territorial waters.

Bermuda was well established as an international financial center. Buttressed by the assimilation of thousands of immigrants, some carefully curated, many very well-heeled, the island nation was able to finance and acquire the critical equipment, materials and human capital/expertise to support her own defense, climate mitigation and health care infrastructure. Bermuda had succeeded where most countries had failed, making Bermuda a very attractive target for migrants. Despite the fact that the island nation was located 600 miles from the nearest land, desperate people will take desperate actions, and the military was constantly on the alert for rogue vessels and unwelcome incursions into their territory. As such, Corey was not expecting to be welcomed with open arms.

The coast guard cutter approached *Mariah* from her starboard quarter and drew alongside, matching *Mariah*'s speed. She was at least four times the size of *Mariah*. Corey couldn't help but notice the 57mm gun mounted on the cutter's foredeck and trained on the catamaran. *Seems like overkill, that gun would sink us in a heartbeat*, Corey registered mentally. Resistance was not a survivable option. Despite the trepidation of staring down the barrel of a powerful automatic weapon, he was relieved that this was a coast guard vessel and not what would certainly have been another, this time fatal, encounter with pirates.

"Sailboat *Mariah*, this is the Bermudian Coast Guard Vessel *Sir Edward Richards*, heave to and prepare to be boarded," the voice on the loudspeaker commanded in that distinctive Bermudian accent that sounds like a hybrid between British and American English. "Have everyone on board the vessel in the cockpit and visible at all times."

Corey nodded and waved that he understood. He went to the helm and disengaged the autopilot. He called out to the Bermudian vessel on the megaphone, "My wife and I are the only two people on board," pointing from Amelia to himself. "We will comply, but I need to turn her into the wind to furl the sails."

"Understood, heave to now."

Corey turned *Mariah* into the wind and furled the sails, as the cutter mirrored his course. They were now heaved to, bobbing in the two-four-foot seas.

"Do you have any weapons?" said the voice on the loudspeaker.

"Yes, we have one pistol," Corey replied.

"Drop it over the side," the voice commanded.

Corey carefully retrieved the pistol and dropped it into the sea.

"You were flying a quarantine flag. Are you ill?"

"No, we used the flag to scare off pirates," Corey explained. "My wife and I are not sick."

"We will wear masks when we come aboard. Stand together and away from the helm."

Corey and Amelia left the helm and moved to the port side of the cockpit. Corey took her hand and she smiled at him. He smiled back.

"Prepare to be boarded."

Here it is, the moment of truth. Will we convince them to let us contact my sister, or will they escort us out of the territorial waters without any consideration? Will this entire trip have been in vain?

Corey and Amelia watched as the Bermudian cutter lowered a Zodiac inflatable boat into the water. The Zodiac carrying five men in uniform approached *Mariah's* starboard quarter, four of the five were heavily armed. One of the men tossed Corey the painter from the Zodiac, which Corey secured to a cleat on *Mariah's* starboard quarter. Three of the men boarded *Mariah* from the stern.

A tall handsome man, apparently in his thirties, appeared to be the officer in charge. "Passports please," he demanded in a Bermudian accent.

Corey produced his passport. "My wife, Amelia, lost her passport in a flood. She has no papers I'm afraid."

The officer looked at Amelia and shook his head as he perused Corey's passport. "You are from the United States?"

"I am from the U.S. My wife is a Canadian citizen," Corey replied.

"Why are you in Bermudian territorial waters?"

"We are seeking asylum. We are fleeing violence and environmental collapse," Corey replied as Amelia nodded in agreement.

"You and over half the planet I'm afraid," the officer replied with a grim look on his face. "We are but a tiny island country, we cannot accept everyone who enters our waters seeking asylum. Bermuda is only accepting asylum seekers under extraordinary circumstances. Do you have any specialized skills that would be of value to our nation, other than your obvious skill in sailing and your courage or foolishness as may be in making this voyage under these conditions?"

"I am a trained and experienced emergency medical technician," Corey replied.

"Ten years Canadian military," Amelia offered in her *Québécois* accent.

Corey looked at Amelia and tried not to show his surprise. *It appears I have much to learn about this remarkable woman.*

"You are French?" The officer asked looking sternly at Amelia.

"*Non*, French Canadian," she replied with a smile.

"And I have relatives already living in Bermuda, my sister, Dr. Kelly Leiter and her husband, Dr. Randy Leiter. I believe they are on staff at the King Edward VII Memorial Hospital," Corey interjected, hoping to change the subject.

The officer turned his attention once more to Corey. "I know Dr. Leiter. She is Chief of Surgery at KEMH. She operated on my mother. She is an excellent surgeon."

"Yes, my sister is a very talented woman." *I hope that the surgery went well and that this man harbors no ill will against my sister.* Corey thought with fingers crossed. *We are either very lucky here, or really screwed.*

"We will contact Dr. Leiter and see if she has a brother named Corey and a sister-in-law named Amelia."

"She does not know about Amelia. We married only a year ago, and I have not spoken with my sister Kelly for over two years. She can certainly vouch for me, and I can vouch for my wife."

The officer looked suspiciously at Amelia and then back again at Corey. "Let's see what Dr. Leiter says. We will consider your request for asylum depending upon her feedback and any other evidence that we can collect from you and your boat. I will ask you one more time," he said, looking sternly first at Corey and then at Amelia, "Do you have any more weapons or any contraband on this vessel?"

"No sir," Corey and Amelia responded almost in unison.

The officer turned away and returned to the Zodiac leaving one armed coast guardsman on board *Mariah*. Corey could see the man talking on the marine radio. Within minutes he climbed back out of the rigid inflatable and on to *Mariah*.

"Dr. Leiter is apparently in the operating theater. We expect that she will return the call from the Duty Officer who will patch her through to me. In the meantime we will conduct a thorough search of this vessel. If we find that you have lied to us, even an appeal from Dr. Leiter will be insufficient and you will be immediately escorted out of Bermudian territorial waters."

"Please proceed with your search." Corey glanced at Amelia who nodded her head, and then back to the officer. "We have nothing to hide. No weapons or contraband on board."

Corey and Amelia sat holding hands in the cockpit as two of the coast guardsmen conducted a thorough search of the boat. They found nothing suspicious other than that the supposed newlyweds apparently did not sleep in the same cabin. After conferring with his subordinates, the officer approached Corey and Amelia. "It has been several years since I was married, but even now my wife and I sleep in the same room. We find it unusual that newlyweds would sleep in separate cabins."

Corey looked at Amelia. She smiled and said "One keeps watch. One sleeps. No time for *l'amour*." She leaned over and kissed Corey on the lips, and he happily kissed her back. She turned to the officer "Soon," as she looked at Corey and winked.

The officer shook his head, but appeared satisfied with the answer, at least for now.

"A call for you Sir." The helmsman of the Zodiac called out, extending his arm holding the radio microphone toward the officer in charge.

The officer returned once more to the Zodiac and spoke briefly on the radio. "We have Dr. Leiter on the radio. She says that she has a brother named Corey, but insists on speaking with you before confirming."

Corey left Amelia's side and quickly made his way to the Zodiac. The helmsman handed the microphone to Corey. "Hello, Kelly?"

"Corey, is that really you?" Kelly Wells Leiter replied on the verge of tears. "I was afraid I'd never see you again."

"I'm here Kel, I'm safe. I missed you so much," Corey also fought back the tears, overjoyed to hear his sister's voice after such a long time.

"Is Sally with you? Captain Paynter said that you were with your wife."

"No Kelly, she fled Sea Isle with her family last summer. I met someone new."

"That was fast," Kelly replied with a surprised inflection in her voice.

"It was truly love at first sight. I will tell you more when we are together again."

"Please give the radio back to Captain Paynter. I will ask him to please allow us to be reunited. Fortunately, I know him well. I operated on his mother, lovely woman, who did very well."

Corey called to Captain Paynter and handed him the microphone. "She asked to speak with you again sir."

Captain Paynter took the microphone from Corey and spoke once more with Kelly Leiter. "Yes Dr. Leiter. Can you confirm that this man is your brother and that this woman is his wife?"

Corey could overhear his sister's voice on the loudspeaker. "Yes Captain, he is my brother. If he says the woman is his wife please believe him. I trust him implicitly."

"Very well then. I will see what I can do with the Immigration Police," Captain Paynter replied. "Good day Dr. Leiter."

Captain Paynter looked at Corey. "I cannot guarantee that you will be accepted, but a recommendation from Dr. Leiter should carry a lot of weight with the Immigration Police. We will tow you in from here. Do you have the yellow Q quarantine flag as opposed to the black and yellow flag that you were flying?"

"We do sir. I will retrieve it from below decks and raise it if that is protocol," Corey replied.

"It is, but first we will bring a tow rope from the *Richards*. Please cleat it to the bow of this vessel." He pointed at the armed man standing at *Mariah*'s starboard quarter. "Guardsman Tucker will remain on board until we are ready to get under way."

Corey replied, "Understood," nodded at Guardsman Tucker and climbed back aboard *Mariah*. Captain Paynter and the Zodiac departed for the mother ship.

Corey went below to retrieve the *Q* flag. The Zodiac was already on its way back to *Mariah* as Corey returned to the cockpit once more. After Corey had received the tow rope and cleated it to *Mariah*'s bow, the Zodiac, including Guardsman Tucker, returned to the *Sir Edward Richards*. Corey raised the *Q* flag and he and Amelia prepared to be towed to what they both hoped would be their safe harbor from the ubiquitous madness and omnipresent catastrophe that they both had endured for so long.

CHAPTER 23

Against the Storm

Corey and Amelia sat and watched as the Islands of Bermuda began to appear on the horizon. A large vessel approached from port, funneling water into its maw like a giant whale shark.

Amelia pointed at the vessel as it passed astern, "*Quoi*? What is that?"

"That appears to be a solar-powered autonomous vessel, cleaning plastic and other debris from the surface. I have seen similar vessels before around Sea Isle, although not any this large. They stopped running as things began to collapse there."

"*Oui*, I remember now, also *en Le Fleuve Saint-Laurent*. Corey *regarder*," Amelia exclaimed pointing to another cleaning vessel off the starboard bow. "Another. *Fantastique*."

"They are cleaning the water. That is fantastic. I wonder how effective they are? Wouldn't it be wonderful if it was once again safe to sail or drive a powerboat without fear of hitting floating debris? If it was safe to drink unfiltered water or eat wild-caught shellfish?" Corey looked at Amelia and shook his head. "If only we could go back in time and correct the mistakes that were made. What I wouldn't give to live in the world of my youth, before the climate collapsed."

"*C'est un beau rêve*, but a beautiful dream."

Corey looked at Amelia and continued his monologue, "For those of us fortunate to have resources, we can find ways to cope with the new reality. *Mariah* has an AI-enabled auto-pilot and forward-looking sonar to avoid flotsam and debris, and a keel guard to deflect debris from the keel. Her jet-powered engines have self-cleaning intake grates and are designed to shunt plastic and other particles away from the engine. Very few vessels are so equipped, making navigation treacherous if not impossible for those less fortunate. The plastic and other debris collects on our once-pristine beaches. It is truly, truly, one disaster after another that humankind has perpetuated on this beautiful planet." Corey looked again at Amelia. "Sorry for my diatribe, but every now and then I have to vent my frustration."

"Diatribe?" Amelia looked at Corey quizzically.

"Ah, sorry, a rant, a verbal release of frustration if you will."

"OK, *je comprends, frustration c'est normal.* So much loss."

"So much tragedy, so much loss indeed." Corey looked away and then back to Amelia.

"But on the bright side, maybe all of the activity we are witnessing is having an effect? Maybe they have solved some of these problems of pollution, at least locally?"

"Hope is all what is left *pour nous*, for us."

Corey looked at Amelia and smiled. *She is so emotionally strong. She deserves to be happy again.* "Hope is something we both share. We will need more than hope however to get through Bermudian customs. We should work on our story more. We need to be in synch. OK?"

"*Oui. Une bonne idée.*"

"As we discussed before, we met when your boat sank near Sea Isle last year and I was one of the first responders who came to your rescue. We fell in love and married shortly thereafter, so married about a year."

Amelia nodded her head.

"We were married online since there was no church, priest or pastor available to marry us. Although satellites were out, online service was available since my house was hardwired."

"OK, sounds *raisonnable*."

"We should probably agree on a wedding date. Let's say our anniversary is June 15th of last year. OK?"

"OK, *le quinze juin*, June 15," she said, nodding her head in agreement.

"No time for a vacation, we spent our honeymoon in Sea Isle, New Jersey."

"OK, Sea Isle, New Jersey," she repeated after Corey.

"We can say that you are a widow, that your husband died when the boat sank. Best to keep things as real as possible to avoid possible slip-ups. Or does that make us sound bad?"

"He died before we meet. Killed by *les pirates*," she said grimly. "He saved *moi*. I left Quebec *après les funérailles. Tout seule*. Alone."

Corey nodded his head. "OK. After we married we decided to leave Sea Isle due to increasing violence and continued deterioration in the climate. We sailed together to Bermuda to start a new life. Sounds good?"

"*Oui*. What about *les détails personnels*? I am thirty-five years. *Les enfants, non*, no kids. *No frères et sœurs*, no brothers or sisters. *Et toi*?"

"Good idea. I am forty-two years old. Also, no children. One sister, Kelly Wells Leiter. Both of my parents are dead. Killed by a drone strike aimed at insurgents."

"So sorry Corey." Amelia looked down momentarily as sadness began to overwhelm her again. "My parents also dead. *La grippe aviare*, the bird flu."

Corey looked at Amelia with sympathy. "I am so sorry. We have both experienced so much tragedy."

"*Oui*, but no more. *Nous devons survivre*. We survive. We live again. *Pour eux*. For them."

"Yes. We owe it to them to carry on."

Amelia and Corey looked forward as the *Sir Edward Richards* towed them closer to Bermuda. Surrounding the islands was a massive wall, a dike measuring at least twenty feet above the surface of the sea.

Amelia pointed at the dike. "Like *le hollandais, Les Pays-Bas*, but more *grand*."

"Yes, I had heard that the Bermudians had recruited Dutch engineers to build them a dike. I had no idea of the scale however. This is an incredible feat of engineering. I guess this is why these islands have survived while so many have been consumed by the sea. They have built a fortress against the storm."

"*C'est incroyable. Fantastique.*"

"That it is. I'm blown away."

The crew of Mariah watched in amazement as a gate opened, allowing the *Richards* and her tow to pass inside the dike. Multiple sluices were apparent in the dike, seemingly allowing the tides and marine life to flow in a regulated manner, while providing a means for controlling the flow of water in or out in an emergency. Once inside the massive barrier an entirely different world was evident. The sea was bustling with sailboats and silent motorized craft of all sizes and configurations. Fishing boats, shrimp trawlers and pleasure craft plied calm azure waters in all directions. It was as if the Tipping Point had never been reached, and life was as it was before the climate catastrophe shattered both their worlds.

Amelia and Corey sat in the cockpit, open-mouthed in amazement.

"Are we dreaming? How can this be?" Corey exclaimed, shaking his head in disbelief.

"*C'est un rêve.* It is a dream. *Un rêve devenu réalité.*"

Corey understood. *This **is** a dream come true.* "No wonder they so carefully protect this place. This is a secret that can't be shared with anyone."

As the *Richards* towed *Mariah* closer to shore, Corey went to the port side railing and peered over the side. Even in the diminished sunlight of late afternoon, he could clearly see the sandy bottom with isolated coral formations and beds of seagrass with starfish and queen conch shells scattered along the ocean floor. Large schools of fish were visible below, their silvery bodies reflecting the light from above.

Amelia appeared at his side. "We can see the bottom even in fifty feet of water," Corey pointed to several large fish seemingly hanging motionless in the water eyeing the schools of jacks and chubs. "Look, those are barracuda."

"So many fish. Good to see." She looked at Corey and smiled. "I concentrate on English now."

Corey smiled back at Amelia, and pointed to the low rolling hills dotted with houses and other buildings. "This is truly spectacular. We are being towed in from the north. Apparently many of the beaches on the south shore have pink sand."

"Pink? *Pourqoui*, sorry, why?"

"Apparently there are small single-celled organisms called foraminifera that live in these waters. Their shells are pink. When they die they wash up on shore and turn the beaches pink."

"Oh, I want to see this."

"You will. We just have to get through customs. I'm sure my sister's position here will help us."

Corey could now clearly see the entrance of the channel leading to the Bermudian Navy Dockyard located at the West End of Bermuda. The calm waters of Stovell Bay and Great Sound were just inside what once was a protective barrier coral reef. Elevated temperatures combined with acidification of the ocean caused by the absorption of massive amounts of carbon dioxide from the atmosphere had killed off most of the coral across the globe. Their calcium carbonate skeletons remained as remnants of the vast living colonies of organisms that once provided shelter and sustenance to reef dwelling fish and invertebrates, as well as protection from high surf, creating natural harbors throughout Earth's tropical and sub-tropical regions. Corey could see the outline of the reef as *Mariah* was towed past the entrance to the channel. *I wonder if there are any living coral here? Coral reefs were a miracle of nature. Now just another casualty of man's willful ignorance.* He shook his head in disgust at man's wanton destruction of God's creation or the natural world. Whatever belief you hold about the origin of the world and the life that inhabits it, the careless destruction of the natural world order was the greatest crime ever perpetrated by humankind.

A rigid inflatable Zodiac approached as they neared the customs dock. A customs agent in the bow called out over a bullhorn: "Ahoy, sailboat *Mariah*. Uncleat yourself from the *Richards*. Do you have a functioning electromagnetic anchor?"

Corey gave the man a thumbs up sign and nodded his head in affirmation.

"Connect to one of the magnetic anchors marked by the yellow buoys."

Amelia went forward and uncleated the tow rope from *Mariah*'s bow. Corey engaged the aqua-jet and maneuvered the catamaran adjacent a yellow buoy. He activated the electromagnetic anchor and it immediately latched on to the magnetic anchor associated with the buoy. *Mariah* was now securely anchored in the customs area of the harbor.

The Zodiac pulled alongside. "You will spend the night here. Customs agents will be with you in the morning." With that, the Zodiac pulled away and zoomed back to the customs dock. Corey and Amelia sat in the cockpit, struggling to control their anxiety while simultaneously brimming with excitement at the chance to start a new life in a microcosm seemingly buffered against the terrible storm that had destroyed virtually all that they knew and had held dear.

CHAPTER 24

The Inquisition

With *Mariah* bobbing gently but securely at anchor in protected waters, Amelia and Corey slept soundly for the first time in weeks. They awoke to bright sunlight shining through the portholes and the sounds of birds singing. They emerged almost simultaneously from their separate cabins and shared the last of Corey's synthetic vanilla latte while seated comfortably in the cockpit.

Beautiful white-feathered egrets, grey-blue herons, and raucous laughing gulls were all clearly visible on shore and in the air. A double-crested cormorant surfaced just off the starboard bow and then quickly dove below the boat in search of breakfast. Corey pointed at a white bird with long wings and longer white tail feathers. "Look Amelia, I believe that is a tropic bird."

Amelia pointed to a flock of majestic birds descending in single file from the sky and skimming over the surface of the sea. "*Regarder* Corey, *les pelicans*."

"Wow. I can't remember the last time I saw a pelican. This is truly unbelievable. It as if this island exists in a time warp, before the climate collapsed around us."

Corey and Amelia turned away from admiring the beauty of nature still preserved in this island paradise to the sound of an approaching Zodiac. The solar battery-powered inflatable with a female customs officer at the helm and a male officer seated just forward of the helm pulled alongside *Mariah*. The seated officer stood, walked forward and handed the painter to Corey, who cleated it off.

"You will be escorted to the customs hall now. Bring your papers, passports, birth certificates, whatever documentation that you have. Apparently one of you, the woman,"

"You mean my wife, Amelia."

"Yes, Amelia, has no documentation. Is this correct?"

"Yes, she lost her identity papers."

"This may be a problem. We will discuss during our interview with you."

Corey uncleated the painter and he and Amelia climbed over the rail and boarded the Zodiac, which immediately sped away to the customs dock. Upon entering the customs house, Amelia and Corey were separated and taken to different rooms for their interviews/interrogations.

It had not occurred to me that we would be separated. Clearly we did not think this all the way through, Corey thought as he was led away from Amelia's side and into a small sterile looking room with a wooden table and two chairs.

"Please be seated Mr. Wells. A customs officer will be with you shortly."

Corey sat and reflected on the situation. *This could be a serious problem. We were so focused on reaching Bermuda that we did not give sufficient thought to what would happen once we arrived. If our stories don't line up we could be denied entry, and this entire trip would have been in vain. Even worse, I don't have any idea as to where we would go. I will not leave her, we cannot return to the United States or Canada, and I do not know of any other safe harbor beyond here.*

A tall, stern-looking female customs officer entered the room. "Good morning Mr. Wells." She said with a strong sing-song Bermudian accent. "May I see your passport and any other papers that you may have?"

Corey presented her with his passport and his birth certificate. "Where is my wife? She lost her identity papers in a flood."

"She is being interviewed in another room. We are aware of the problems with her identity. Your sister, Dr. Leiter, says that you are an experienced emergency medical technician, and have participated in many offshore rescue operations. Is this true?"

"Yes, in addition to my onshore activities with the Cape May County Fire Department and EMS, I assisted the U.S. Coast Guard in offshore search and rescue operations. As the weather became more and more unpredictable and the storms became more intense it seemed more of my time was spent offshore than on. Amelia's, my wife's, boat, *La Dolce Vita*, was just one of many I'm afraid."

"You are obviously a skilled sailor. Although it appears that your boat is very well equipped, state-of-the-art in fact, this journey from the United States was no doubt difficult, especially this time of year. How did you find Bermuda without satellite navigation for example?"

"I learned to navigate by dead reckoning as a teenager. My parents wanted us to be self-sufficient and to not rely exclusively on technology. They were somewhat prescient. They saw the threats, not only from climate change, but also from physical and cyber-attacks from foreign adversaries and even from AI, artificial intelligence, itself. They built a house that was state-of-the-art, but, other than being hardwired for access to the internet, was essentially off the grid."

"Very good, she said, nodding her head. You clearly know how to sail. Did you encounter any storms or pirates during your journey?"

"I, we, encountered both during our trip. We managed to survive a powerful storm by shortening sail and carefully steering the boat at a forty-five-degree angle to the waves so as to reduce the risk of broaching or capsizing the boat."

The customs officer seemed impressed with Corey's knowledge and apparent seamanship.

"We also escaped from pirates who almost captured us, but we were able to disable their vessel using an underwater drone to wrap a cable around their propeller. It was an old-style fossil-fuel powered inboard engine."

"Sounds like quite an adventure Mr. Wells. Most who try and reach these shores fail. You are here, so that in and of itself speaks to your skill and capabilities."

"My wife also has significant skill and seamanship. She played a critical role in our survival on this voyage. She too has a lot to offer this community."

"We shall see. I will speak to her and then return to follow-up with you." With that she departed the interview room and closed the door behind her.

Corey tried hard to control his anxiety. What seemed like an eternity passed before the officer returned to the room.

"There are some inconsistencies between Ms. Lavoie's story and yours."

Corey tried to prevent his face from showing his concern. *So her last name is Lavoie. How did I not think to ask her that? We were so busy surviving and grieving we obviously did not really get to know each other.*

The officer continued, "For example, why do you not have the same last name?"

"In Quebec, where she comes from, the women typically do not change from their maiden names when they get married."

"Why do you not have tan lines on your ring fingers?"

"We were running from pirates and did not want to show any jewelry or other signs of wealth. We only put them on again when we knew we had reached Bermudian waters."

The customs officer looked Corey in the eyes. "She said that she lost her papers when her boat sank. You said that she lost them in a flood."

Corey hesitated for a moment. *Think fast Corey, think fast.* "All I know is that she lost her papers before we met. It is true that her sailboat capsized and sank in a storm. I was part of a team that rescued her and that is how we met. We never discussed when she lost her papers, just that they were gone."

The officer stopped and thought for a moment. Her face revealed no sign as to whether or not she was satisfied with Corey's response. She continued, "Bermuda is a carefully kept secret, for obvious reasons. We are a small island nation and cannot absorb any more immigrants. How did you know of us, and why did you come here?"

"I think that you know the answer to that. I came because of my sister. She is my last living relative."

"And Ms. Lavoie?"

"She came with me."

"She says she came to start a new life in a safe place."

"Yes, we both did."

"Her English is not very good. What do you really know about her, other than she is a very physically attractive woman?"

"She understands English perfectly well. I speak some French and understand more than I speak. It is true that we do not have a long history together, but in addition to being physically attractive, as you say, she is smart, strong, kind and very capable."

"Your sister, who is a very highly valued member of our community, says that she will vouch for you, but she does not know Amelia Lavoie."

I will not throw her under the bus here. I owe it to her and I owe it to JP. "We are married. I love her and will not abandon her."

The officer looked at Corey without showing any emotion or reaction to Corey's explanations. "Your sister, Dr. Leiter, is here. She would like a word with you."

The officer opened the door, and motioned for Kelly to enter the room, after which she closed the door and walked down the hall.

Kelly could barely control her emotions upon seeing her brother. Corey stood and crossed the room to hug her, tears streaming down his cheeks.

"Corey, Corey, Corey, I thought you were gone. We heard that things were bad in the United States. I thought I'd never see you again," she said, her voice choked with emotion.

"Things are very bad Kel, bad enough for me to decide to make this trip at the tail end of hurricane season. I hadn't talked to you, and had no way to reach you, but you are my only lifeline. But I am here now, I made it."

Corey pulled away and took a look at his sister. "You look great. Chief of Surgery, Wow!"

"Bermuda has been good to me. Randy and I definitely made the right choice moving here before everything went south and the world turned upside down. We have one child, a two-year old girl, and are planning another."

"Fantastic. I have a niece. I can't wait to meet her," he said excitedly. Then his face suddenly turned serious. *Don't want to be presumptuous here, maybe they won't let us in.* "Of course, they have to let me enter the country first. Do you know where we stand on this?"

"I think they are OK with admitting you on the strength of my endorsement. However, I do not know this woman. I knew your fiancé Sally of course, she was a good person, but I do not know this Amelia. I am uncomfortable vouching for someone I don't know."

"You have to trust my judgement here Kelly, I would not fall in love with someone who was not worthy of it."

"I am trusting you here Corey. Are you sure that you trust her? If this woman turns out to be a problem you and she will both be banished, and I will never see you again."

"Not only do I love her Kel, I owe her my life. She saved me from a pirate who had boarded *Mariah*. A pirate who was preparing to shoot me."

"Saved you how?" Kelly asked.

"She shot him with my pistol as he was taking aim at me. She is a good person, I am sure of that. She is brave and strong, but also kind and gentle. I will not abandon her."

"OK Corey. You are my brother and I will do everything I can to help you, and her, to be admitted to this country."

"Thank you Kelly. Whatever happens, know that I love you, I am proud of you, and I want only the best for you and your family."

Corey and Kelly hugged again, strong emotions once more welling up inside them, tears filling their eyes. Kelly pulled away, left the interview room, and disappeared down the hall.

The customs officer returned with Amelia in tow. Amelia sat next to Corey. They held hands waiting to hear the verdict that would determine the course of their lives from here on out.

The officer looked at Corey, then Amelia, then back at Corey, a stern expression on her face. Finally, she spoke, "You will be released into the custody of Dr. Leiter at least until your probationary period of two years has been satisfied. You both must find suitable employment or have a child in that time frame to remain here. If either of you breaks the law or runs afoul of our customs, one or both of you will be expelled from Bermuda. Permanently. Do you understand?"

Amelia and Corey looked at each other, trying to control their elation. They looked back at the officer, nodded their heads in agreement and said "Yes, thank you so much" more or less in unison.

The customs officer continued. "You will remain aboard your vessel for one more day. We can provide provisions if you need them. Dr. Leiter is making arrangements for you to dock your vessel at the Bermuda Yacht Club in Hamilton. You can remain there permanently or until you find land-based accommodations, which are in short supply here as you may know. If you successfully complete your probationary period you will both be issued new identity papers and a Bermudian passport."

Corey and Amelia looked at each other, then back at the officer, shared joy plastered on both their faces. "We cannot thank you enough. We will not disappoint you or the Bermudian authorities," Corey exclaimed excitedly.

"We make you proud," Amelia said, beaming with happiness.

The officer smiled and opened the door. "Please come with me and I will escort you back to your boat." She led Corey and Amelia out of the customs house and to the Zodiac that would carry them back to *Mariah*. She then turned to Corey and said, "Good luck to you Mr. Wells. I wish you and your wife health, happiness and success in Bermuda."

Amelia left Corey's side and hugged the customs officer. "Thank you, thank you." The officer at first looked surprised, and then smiled at both Corey and Amelia as they boarded the Zodiac for the short ride back to their floating home.

CHAPTER 25

Dénouement

Corey and Amelia stood in *Mariah*'s cockpit, watching as the sun set in spectacular hues of red, orange and purple over the West End of Bermuda.

Corey took Amelia's hands in his. He stood before her and looked her in the eyes. *I want to gaze into these beautiful eyes for the rest of my life. I love this woman with all of my heart, but I must let her be free.* "Amelia, I had an obligation to Jean-Pierre, a promise to keep you safe and deliver you to Bermuda." *I promised JP posthumously, but it was my obligation none-the-less.* "You, we, are finally safe.

In the process I find that I've fallen in love with you. In fact, I've loved you since we first met." Corey could not read the expression on Amelia's face—was it sympathy, love, or confusion? "But I have no expectation that you will love me in return. We have roles to play for now, but at some point you will want to live your own life, and I will not hinder you or stand in your way. Despite these rings on our fingers you have no obligation to me other than to live free and be happy."

Amelia looked at Corey with tears welling in her eyes. "Corey, this has been *très rapide pour moi*, for me. It is *trop tôt*, too soon. I grieve Jean-Pierre."

Corey nodded his head, his eyes also filling with tears. "I understand."

"*Mais*, you Corey, you are *fort*, you are strong, you are *gentil*, you are *vrai*, honest and true. You are also *beau*, eh, handsome." She let go of Corey's right hand and put her hand over her heart. "I know, *dans mon coeur*, I will love you. Please give me some time."

With that she reached up and kissed Corey lightly on the lips. And for that brief moment in time all was right with the world.

THE END

Acknowledgements

I would like to thank my beta readers, Ed Hennemann, Mark Gambler and Sharon Mostyn who read earlier drafts and provided substantive comments and feedback. Good people all.

Thanks to my family, Michelle, Jeffrey and Nicole for being my anchor in fair weather and in foul, and for enriching my life immeasurably.

Finally, I would like to acknowledge my parents, who provided constant love and support and raised me to see the world not only how it is, but also how it should be.

About the Author

W.W. Hennemann is an award-winning author and novelist. He has a PhD in Zoology from the University of Florida and forty years of experience in academia and the medical device industry.

W.W. has a lifelong passion for and fascination with the natural world in general and the sea in particular. He has skippered sailboats in and around Florida and the Bahamas, including several sometimes serene, sometimes harrowing, crossings of the Gulf Stream and the Florida Straits.

W.W. has numerous scientific publications and medical device patents to his name and likes to infuse his writing with snippets of biological and scientific fact and conjecture. He has traveled to every continent, lived in four states and three countries, and currently resides with his family in Bucks County, Pennsylvania.

This is his first published novel.

Visit the author online at www.wwhennemann.com.